A
KILLING IN
REAL ESTATE

A KILLING IN REAL ESTATE

Frank Orenstein

ST. MARTIN'S PRESS/NEW YORK

Design by Eric Baker Design

Library of Congress Cataloging-in-Publication Data

Orenstein, Frank.
    A killing in real estate.
    "A Thomas Dunne book."
    I. Title.
PS3565.R39K5   1989   813'.54   88-29883
ISBN 0–312–02596-3

First Edition

10 9 8 7 6 5 4 3 2 1

For Bob, and also for Naranja and the rest of
the dubious crew

CHAPTER 1

A Killing
in Real Estate

AS HARRIET LORIMER always said, it depends on your point of view. A bird's-eye view of Appleboro, or perhaps the view from a plane some 10,000 feet up, would have encompassed, according to the time of year and whether or not the trees were in leaf, the white stone face of the cliffs lying to the north and west, the irregular courses of roads that skirted the steepest hills and paid appropriate deference to the areas most likely to be flooded by the Shawangunk Kill in spring, and the fields of apple trees laid out across the town as evenly and rigidly as if they were part of a picture drawn by an insecure ten-year-old in search of certainty.

Come down a bit and transform that sky-high plane into a crop duster. The houses, not recognizable from higher up, are more apparent now. The old farmhouses, with sagging roofs over rotted beams, held together as much by inertia as by nails, sit amid the cornfields and the orchards. Stone houses, some going back three centuries, come into view. These, either still maintained by the original families or sold as a piece of history to ex-urbanites from New York City needing to be relieved of their excess

1

wealth, are in prime condition; no shingles need replacing and no paint is peeling off the frames around the sparkling windows of purplish antique glass.

The A-frames and cottages occupied by weekenders up from the big city two hours to the south, standing on plots from one to one hundred acres, the specific sizes being directly proportional to the bank balances of the owners, will be noted, as will the artificial ponds disported about many of these properties. Over time, some of these visitors will grow old and retire to Appleboro, seeking space and air and quiet while still remaining reasonably close to the decreasingly attractive amenities of New York City. From your crop duster you will see that the houses of the retirees lack vegetable gardens; only weekenders are foolish enough to grow their own provender, an activity that gives them a false sense of security and the misguided belief that their aching backs will somehow make them at one with Nature.

Your plane flies on. Suddenly, a curious rash: Tract homes, modular machines for living, erector set shelters for young families whose nesting instincts crowd the limits of their pocketbooks, begin to spread before you as evenly as the apple trees. They look as if some great plastic bird of evil intent had flown again and again over the town and deliberately, maliciously, deposited its dreary plastic turds at regular intervals without regard to trees, hills, swamps, brooks, or neighbors, the better to urbanize the environment.

Now land and proceed afoot. You were wrong from above; the plastic homes are not totally identical, not quite. Some attempts have been made, either by the developers or the buyers, to achieve a measure of individuality. Sometimes it works. And sometimes a misguided creativity will turn a house into an Abe Lincoln cabin with pseudologs glued on to the front and sides (but not on to the rear), or into a plantation house lacking only Scarlett O'Hara, cotton fields, and banjo-strumming slaves. And that's at best;

2

other times the styles are more difficult to categorize, and can only be described as something built by the blind. Most of the construction is decent, but too much is thrown up by speculators who know the young buyers plan an occupancy of only a handful of years, following which they fully expect to move up in the world. It can be said of these latter homes that even the field mice, searching for draftproof shelter in winter, frequently disdain tenancy after the first few weeks.

The roads have been similarly adapted. Georgie's Old Ford Landing, a path to the river, is now Fairview Lane. And off to one side of Vista Trail, the dirt road that ambles down to Woody Dell Acres, you can find, hidden in the grass, an older, half-obliterated sign for Deaf Jones Road. It used to lead to Swamp Bottom.

Finally, get even closer to the ground for another kind of bird's-eye view, this time a crow's. The crow is not happy. Each year brings him and his kinfolk less space in which to be undisturbed. And even more to the point, the crow is poking about in a cavity in which he knows there is supposed to be something good to eat. The crow is an ideal exemplar of behavioral psychology: Poke in a hole and get something to eat and be happy; do it many times and be conditioned to expect happiness through poking in a hole. Then poke in the hole and find no food and be frustrated and unhappy and headed for a nervous breakdown. The hole is one of a matching pair in a modest expanse of hard, white surface. There are other holes as well, but these are of no particular concern to the crow. The hole of choice was once filled with something edible and even totally delicious, if a bit viscous. As the crow would not have been in the least interested to learn, it had been, in its day, an eye, a blue eye, one of the two blue eyes that used to occupy the matching holes in the hard, white surface.

CHAPTER 2

March 21: Pussy Willows, Onion Grass

APPLEBORO WAS, IN the last analysis, a series of mistakes compounded by time, disinterest, and enthusiastically ignorant scholarship. It had been founded in the seventeenth century by a Dutchman named Appel, who hadn't realized at the time that he was founding anything. His children called it Appelburg, in honor of their beloved progenitor, but the English conquerors corrected what they regarded as an inability of colonials to do anything right, and the town became Appleburgh, the final *h* establishing proper usage as it was regarded in the mother country.

During World War I, in an access and excess of patriotic fervor, a local history teacher at the consolidated high school down Route 299 announced that the final syllable betrayed Teutonic, or Hunnish, roots, and by unanimous vote of the town council, Appelburg, which had become Appleburgh, became Appleboro. This name remained, not because of a growing maturity on the part of the inhabitants but because, frankly, nobody gave much of a damn. The population had peaked at 1,100 in the days of riverboat traffic, when the Erie Canal took the produce of the west down to New York City, and when the Delaware and Hudson Canal funneled the coal of Pennsylvania to the stoves and furnaces of the big town. But the railroads and then the trucks and the airplanes took over, and Appleboro limped along on the produce of its orchards and by serving as a bedroom for people who worked in the larger towns but wanted someplace sleepy to sleep in.

Until the Big Apple to the south reached out its tentacles and started moving in. Until *New York* magazine announced its discovery that the Appleboro area was inexpensive, available, and ripe for the picking. Until the federal highway program provided two major roads, one going north-south, the other east-west, that crossed each other only a few miles from the Appleboro general store.

Sooner or later, the month of March brings a day in May, however briefly. This year it came on March 21, appropriately enough the first day of spring. Harriet Lorimer was on the patio, her favorite and rather ratty cardigan pulled tightly around a body she preferred thinking of more as comfortable than as overweight, her eyes shut and her face pointed up at the sun, somewhat in the manner of an antique sunflower. "Oh, God, that feels good."

"I know it does, Mother," Ed said, "and I wish you'd let yourself have more of it. It would make Virginia and me rest a lot easier." Harriet's son and his wife were up from New York for their first visit of the year to see how their mother and mother-in-law had weathered the winter.

"Not again, Ed. Not again. I'm not selling the house and I'm not moving to Florida. Not while I can still waddle on my own. Now that's an end to it." To signify finality, she got up from her chair and pointed her field glasses down the road. "You know, the first day I can go out with these glasses and see what's happening, it's the first day of the year for me, and—I think I can see some onion grass, but that's about all. And," she added, shifting

5

slightly, "some pig has dumped garbage in the Beldings' field again. Here, take a look at that, will you!"

Dutifully, her son took the field glasses and focused them on the next property. "You mean that bright blue patch next to the hickory? Jason'll spiral up when he sees it. When's he due back?"

"Oh, any week now, I expect. He feels about Florida the way I do, but with his arthritis, he's got no choice. Every damn winter for the last half-dozen years. Since Betty died. Just after your father went, it was."

"He could get a pile for his place, too, Ma."

Virginia said, "Leave your mother alone. It's her decision."

"Christ! I didn't say anything!"

"Thank you, Virginia," Harriet said. "Between us, someday we'll get him trained." She turned to her son. "Do you realize what Carl Van Houten wants to do with Jason's land? First of all, Van Houten's bought up two hundred landlocked acres behind Jason from the Oostdyks. No access to the road, but the original patent on the land guarantees right of passage to the Oostdyks and their heirs in perpetuity to use the wagon road across Jason's for getting firewood up behind him."

"Okay. So? So this Van Houten's got a right-of-way. What's the big deal?"

Harriet looked at her son critically. "I always knew when we let you go to business school, you'd end up a Tory, boy. Probably end up gentrifying a couple of hundred Puerto Ricans out of their homes before you're done."

"You tell him, Mother," Virginia put in.

"I'll tell you what's the big deal," Harriet went on. "First, Van Houten figures on building two hundred condos on that land. Ruin the whole damn town. Second, a right-of-way for the Oostdyks to get firewood doesn't mean a public road across Jason Belding's land. Third, you know the town board of this cruddy town—"

"Mustn't swear, Momma," Ed said, trying to turn off the stream with a joke.

6

"Cruddy town," Harriet repeated firmly. "Who's willing to serve on the board of a cruddy little town? Just the big landowners and the developers and they don't do anything except take in each other's washing; and what do they do, they say sure, great, build your condos, the road across Belding's land is a terrific idea, why not put in a four-lane highway and happy days are here again!" She flung her arms up in disgust.

"Well, if Belding doesn't like it, he can always go to court, can't he?"

"That's exactly what he's done. But meantime, that sneak Van Houten has had his bulldozers and work crews and whatnot up there and he's actually started building! You know what's likely to happen next. It'll drag through the courts and the decision will be that it was wrong to build, but then there'll be the plea of hardship because he's already done it. Then it'll go to another court and Jason'll run out of money or die and his boy will be only too delighted to drop the whole thing if Van Houten will buy his land, too! That'll be great for me, won't it? Probably put me between a bowling alley and a massage parlor." She snorted, indignant in advance of the offense.

"Like I say, Ma, now's the time to sell out."

Harriet stared down the valley. She watched a hawk riding the updrafts toward the cliff. Her eyes turned down toward last year's pine needles, brown and prickly, on the equally brown lawn. She looked at the muddy patches on the side of her driveway, soft, soggy, quiet patches of good earth. She looked at her son. "I don't know who you are, boy. Not my son, that's for sure. Your pa must have fathered you on some other woman. Probably some stuffed brassiere of a Huguenot like Judith Oostdyk. That's it, I think. La Oostdyk is your mother, and they passed you off on me while I was asleep."

"Right on, Mother," Virginia cheered.

"I don't know for sure what that means, my dear, but thank you. Let's go in and have a scotch and get ourselves away from this Oostdyk bastard."

"You sure he's a bastard, Mother?"

"Pretty sure. No husband of mine could have married an Oostdyk woman, not even to get into the Settlers Club."

The two women linked arms and headed inside for a drink. Ed Lorimer shook his head and looked down the valley for a last time that day. What was so special? he wondered. Trees, cliffs, weeds, and a pile of bright blue garbage on the Belding land.

CHAPTER 3

March 27: Coltsfoot

JUDITH OOSTDYK, NÉE Janvier, was at age fifty the same handful of pounds overweight as Harriet Lorimer, and about the same height, as well. There the resemblance stopped. Where Harriet projected the comfortable though slightly mushy warmth of a Brahms lullaby, Judith was more of a Wagnerian blast from the trombones; it would have been easy to imagine her in the horned helmet provided by a second-string Bavarian opera house, carrying a spear and appearing somewhere between awesome and absurd as she stood at the edge of a crag and hooted.

Henry Oostdyk, in contrast, was thin, gentle, and played out. His progenitors had been on the land since the 1600s, and for some reason, possibly related to radon deposits in the soil, the family had been growing thinner of wrist and blood ever since those early heroic times. Henry kept himself to the lee side of life, as much as possible untouched, like a mummy under wraps. And like a mummy, he was frozen in time, his face growing sere and wrinkled, but otherwise unmarked, fixed in a bright-eyed adolescence that convinced every young woman in Appleboro that he must have been a knockout when he was young.

The Oostdyks lived, to Judith's intense satisfaction,

in the seventeenth-century Oostdyk House, open to public viewing on Settlers Day once a year on payment of a small but definitely involuntary contribution to the Settlers Club Restoration Fund. (Many elderly couples attended, the ladies sucking in air in admiration and wonder, their husbands blowing air out in resignation and boredom.) The house and its furnishings were models of grace and elegance, though a shade shabbier than Judith would have preferred. She tried to tell herself that shabbiness was a mark of gentility; the Roosevelt place over in Hyde Park was certainly shabby, and those Roosevelts were newcomers to the Hudson Valley compared to the Oostdyks. But she knew that the problem was money. Money and Henry's family bank, of which he was the sole and unfortunate owner.

They were at table. Judith did the cooking, but they still set the good service out on the long table in the formal dining room, the way they did when help came in to serve a larger gathering on occasional weekends. "Listen, Henry," Judith said, "I think we can dispense with a big trip this fall. We did England and Holland last year, and after all, I don't know why a leaf weekend or two in Maine or New Hampshire wouldn't do us as well. For a change, you know?"

"You're a sweetheart," Henry said. "And I know. But don't you worry. It'll all be different once Carl Van Houten takes over that parcel up the mountain."

"If he takes it, you mean. If only that Belding ass wasn't so stubborn." She stabbed resentfully at a morsel of filet of sole that she had bought Sunday morning at the Shoprite. (No one she knew would have seen her shopping for fish in a supermarket at that hour, instead of patronizing the more expensive fish market.) Frozen fish, she thought, glumly; I wonder whether there's really a difference or whether I've just talked myself into it.

"Please, dear. I promise you. We've got the right to traffic over Belding's land, and the courts will recognize

10

that even if the deed says it's to get firewood from the mountain. Things change, things they couldn't have guessed at back then, and then, well, well, you know." He petered out weakly. Two hundred acres at almost five thousand dollars an acre and he and Judith would be set. He could let someone else take over the bank. The area was growing, and one of the big outfits down in New York would snap it up. Surely they would. They had to.

And he had to change the subject. "The Spingle man was in the bank again the other day. Wants another extension on his mortgage."

"Oh? And?"

"Oh, I suppose we'll let him have it. He's good for it. The way things are going around here, all the new building and everything, a plumber's bound to make a decent living. Soon as he connects."

Judith set down her fork; the filet turned to ashes in her mouth, its remains a tortured, soggy mass on her plate. She sighed. "You're too damned soft with these people, Henry. The way things are going around here, Spingle'll drink the place dry, that's what. You should foreclose; that land is valuable." She stabbed a frozen pea and looked resentfully at a congealed spot of egg she had overlooked when she had done the plates after breakfast. "I could kill that Belding," she announced.

"Don't talk like that, Judy." Henry's voice was tired. "Somebody could hear you talk like that. Please don't."

"'Somebody could hear you talk like that,'" Judith mimicked. "Who?" she asked. She waved a fork around the room. "The servants? The gardener? The guests?" She put her fork down. "Oh, Henry, Henry, sometimes you make me sick."

CHAPTER 4

April 8: Dame's Rocket

AFTER THE LAST of the stragglers had left the library, inevitably letting the screen door slam, Elfrida Von Hesse went slowly into her office and sagged into the swivel chair. Of course, it wasn't exactly an office, but Elfie had, all by her lonesome, with a minor assist from the cleaning woman, shoved four filing cabinets and a bookcase into position to section off a corner of the main room. When one of the busybodies on the library board had questioned her action, she explained, more snippily than a town librarian should have, "It isn't simply to satisfy my vanity, Mrs. Van Nuys, but if my position is to have any authority at all, it needs some of the trappings of office. The president doesn't ride down Pennsylvania Avenue in a second-hand Hyundai, you know, even if that would get him where he's going just as handily." She had, at that moment, sniffed. No one bothered to contradict; it didn't matter enough.

Elfie had become the town librarian, or, as she put it, had taken the post of town librarian, over twenty-five years ago, right out of school with a degree in library science. Even then concerned with the significance of the assignment, she had affected a hairstyle that culminated in a

12

forbidding, feltlike wad, suitable for poking pencils into, on top of her head. She was a timid girl, though less so than she thought, and told those who hinted at the potential benefits of a stylistic reconsideration, "I know it's 1910-ish, but it'll help me keep order when so many of the kids who come in are only a few years younger than I am." The explanation no longer applied, but the symbol remained, solidified by custom.

Silence settled over the three-room operation as palpably as the dust that drifted down onto the books through the undisturbed air. Elfrida felt the customary end-of-day relief as that little headache behind the eyes started to subside. It had been a hard day. Books were lost or late; books were returned to the shelves incorrectly; borrowers avoided their fines. (Actually the day had been precisely like any other day.) The return of warm weather gave hope, but nevertheless, it had been a hard day.

She drew a lined yellow pad from under the box of tissues in her top-left drawer, and in a crabbed handwriting headed the first page: Spring, 1989. She began to sketch out those current events suitable for preservation in the updated history of Appleboro. The honorary post of town historian had quite naturally fallen to her when the preceding incumbent had been summoned by the Lord to grace the Huguenot platoon of His Band of Angels, and it was an assignment, though unpaid, that gave more pleasure to the woman than did her salaried position. For one thing, she sincerely loved the little town, and for another, she gained entry into the lives and social activities of the Dutch and Huguenot gentry whose history she was in effect recording. (More recent arrivals and summer people were noted in the historical records as population statistics rather than as individuals, the few exceptions being the occasional creative artists of more than local reputation who had strayed into the area, sniffed the air, and, finding it good, had settled in for a lifetime or until the next divorce.)

She nibbled the eraser on the end of the pencil. In

13

this year (she wrote), finis was writ to a chapter in the history of Appleboro when the very last of the seventeenth-century Dutch holdings at the base of the Shawangunk cliffs passed from the hands of the original family to a private developer. Elfie smiled ruefully; it was a sad thing that the Oostdyks had had to relinquish the land, but there was consolation in the fact that the moment fell during her tenure as historian and could be recorded by her. Or would be recorded by her whenever Jason Belding got back from Florida and started behaving himself.

Florida, she thought. The times were indeed out of joint, as the Bard had put it. In the autumn, for some odd reason, no one in town had died, not even the elderly. Not a soul. The local funeral parlor director was going insane, since the old folk had only started passing on after they had departed for the winter to the warmth and trashy glitz of Florida, where their remains were converted into cold cash by alien necropolitan enterprises.

Something was wrong somewhere. No funerals; the Oostdyks being written out of the Romance of the Shawangunks. Heaven knew what the rest of the year might bring. The signs were bad. It was enough to make a body sick, simply sick!

CHAPTER 5

April 8: Gill-Over-the-Ground

MELVIN SPINGLE, ELEVEN years old and distinguished only by an ability to break his father's heart, was seated at the table in the family kitchen, wincing less at his father's words than at the fetid waves of beer on which the words were wafted in his direction. He kicked mechanically at the table leg.

"And stop kicking the goddamn table, you hear me? I try to talk some sense into the boy and all I get out of him is—What's he trying to do, smash it up I got to buy a new one?"

Ellie Spingle looked over from the sink. "Stop it, George. Leave the boy alone. That table was falling apart when we got it out of a yard sale ten years ago, and you know it. Besides, that's not what's got your goat anyway, so simmer down."

George Spingle thought. "You know, you're right. What's got me going is this boy's stories, always these damn stories. He's making a laughingstock of us all over town."

"You're not doing so bad yourself," Ellie retorted. "Down at the deli, they're waiting for you to get yourself a

15

hernia dragging the empties back every Saturday. Besides, the boy hasn't done anything."

Melvin whimpered slightly, playing up to the chance to grab a slice of sympathy from his ma. "I didn't do nothin', Daddy," he said weakly.

"Yeah, you didn't do nothin'. Not a thing. Don't play baseball, don't play catch, don't work around the house, just make up stories. Last week you tell your teacher you saw an eagle carry off a baby. In its claws, for God's sake! That's not bad enough, you're down the police station yesterday. A skeleton in a field this time, crows pecking at flesh, God knows what else. Jimmy Tierney comes over from the station, says I ought to do something about you. Last week the school psychologist calls your mother in. School psychologist! What I oughta do is paddle your tail, kid. I'm too soft on you, is what." He lifted his beer bottle to his face, gurgled, and belched.

But it was true: Melvin Spingle, gentle eyes behind large glasses, skinny and pale of skin, didn't do anything much. They used to force him to play baseball in school— the school psychologist had flunked him on socialization— but he only got on base once, when the pitcher hit him with the ball, at which Melvin fell down in surprise while the rest of the players collapsed in laughter. That got him a free base, but later in the inning, when he was rounding third, he stopped to lunge after a toad of special merit and was tagged out. Since then, he had three times run away when it was time to choose up teams, and by tacit agreement, the school authorities made the decision to be unaware of his absence.

Melvin did well in school, and probably had the talent to lead the class, but the notion of being the best frightened him. It invited retribution of some dimly perceived variety, and the boy generally settled for coming in fourth or fifth, just behind the honor students. So, though Daddy wouldn't have put it that way, he achieved distinction only in his imagination. Baby-toting eagles, skeletons in fields,

16

and once a maiden tied to a tree and suffering the lash, though on further questioning, it was revealed that Melvin wasn't exactly sure of what a maiden was, other than something that shouldn't be tied to a tree, much less suffer the lash.

"Listen, son," George Spingle said, "you don't want people to say you're crazy, do you?"

"No, Daddy," Melvin said weakly, kicking at the table again until he suddenly stopped and looked fearfully at his father.

An idea penetrated George's alcoholic haze. "Melvin," he asked sternly, "you been playing around?"

"I don't know what you mean, Daddy."

"You know what I mean. Playing around with yourself. A boy could go crazy that way. You know that? Boys lose their minds they play around with theirselves."

"Stop that!" Ellie snapped. "You've got no right talking to the child like that! Shut up, damn it!"

"Well, it's true. There's got to be something going on. You want the kid to end up nutty as Tillie Jessup? That what you want, huh?"

Melvin looked back and forth from one of his parents to the other, as if he were at a tennis match, unlikely though that might have been. He lacked the slightest idea of what they were talking about. "Ma," he asked, "could I watch television now, maybe?"

His mother ignored him. "Oh, George, George," she said sadly, "sometimes you make me sick."

CHAPTER 6

April 10: Purple Violet

IT WAS EVENING, and chilly. Art Jessup built a small fire and he and Matilda sat in front of it, he in the Morris chair with the threadbare upholstery, she in the Windsor rocker, on the seat a needlepoint cushion that she had made from a kit. The doctor had said needlepoint might calm her nerves, help her settle down. The cat rubbed himself ecstatically across her leg.

"Bobby coming home soon?" she asked.

"Later," her husband answered, and sick with love, he looked at her, her gray hair in a neat bun in back, her thin hands folded in her lap, and her wide, trusting gray eyes turned on him. "Later, I guess."

"Oh." She rocked her chair. "When, later?"

"Maybe tomorrow?"

She stopped rocking. "Tomorrow! Bobby not coming home tonight?"

"Maybe tonight, then. But later." It was easier that way. Besides, she didn't remember from one minute to the next. "Til," he asked, "how'd you like to get away from here, someplace warm. Florida, maybe."

She shook her head. "Got to wait for Bobby."

"No use working a farm around here anymore. Not

like when we were young. Taxes too high. We could get a place, maybe a little pool. Someplace warm. Tired of huddling around a fire. You, too?"

She thought, frowning. "Maybe a little. A little, maybe." A moment later she asked, "Bobby, too?"

"Sure. Bobby, too. You want a cup of tea? I'll make a couple of cups." He got up and lumbered into the kitchen, and after he put the water on, he leaned heavily over the sink and shook his head. When the kettle whistled, he blew his nose noisily, poured the water into the teapot, put the pot, two cups, and the carton of low-fat milk on the tray they had bought at the county fair forty years before, and returned to the living room.

"We'll let it steep a bit," he said. "Anyway, looks to me like Van Houten's going to have to give up on the Oostdyk land, this lawsuit and all, and we'd get a right good price for this place."

But Til wasn't listening. Her eyes were blank and she sat rigidly in her chair. "They'll be punished," she said. "They keep Bobby away from home, they'll be punished." Then, in a voice not hers, she intoned, "'For I the Lord thy God am a jealous God, visiting the iniquity of the fathers upon the children unto the third and fourth generation of them that hate me.'"

Art said, "Listen, Til, that old snoop Stoddard'll be stopping by to pick up some of your preserves this evening. Why don't you let me take care of him, hey? You just sit quiet."

She sat quiet, but she added, "'As silver is melted in the midst of the furnace, so shall ye be melted in the midst thereof; and ye shall know that I the Lord have poured out my fury upon you.'" The cat jumped onto her lap as she spoke, adding body warmth to the warmth of the fire to arrive at something near cat heaven. But Matilda's body was rigid and she rocked as she chanted, and, unaware, she stroked the animal with an increasingly mechanical harshness until it hissed in annoyance and left to resettle on the hearth. Outside, the wind keened in the chimney in hollow response to the threatening biblical passages.

"Oh, Til, sometimes I feel so sick," her husband murmured.

CHAPTER 7

April 11: Trout Lily

*B*EN STODDARD, LOCAL schoolteacher by profession and local snoop by preference, did indeed show up that evening to buy some of Matilda Jessup's tomato pickles (leftover jars from the previous season), but though he pointed his needle nose in every direction and sniffed like a beast of the field, nostrils on the twitch, Art Jessup kept him from picking up anything but the pickles. This left him with no excuse to get on the horn and tell a confidant of choice about poor dear Matilda Jessup and how sorry he was, and wasn't Art Jessup a saint on earth to put up with it, and "Heaven knows I'd never be able to do it myself."

That much was entirely true; he'd never have been able to do it himself. Stoddard had been selflessly dedicated to Stoddard for seventeen years, after his wife had walked out and, for all Ben knew or cared, had headed for outer space. He had been dimly aware that the United Parcel truck had been coming up the driveway with an increasing frequency, though there hadn't been any corresponding increase in monthly bills. The slight and uninteresting mystery was solved one day when the truck arrived and, instead of leaving a parcel, picked up Mrs. Stoddard, three suitcases, and an overstuffed laundry bag and disappeared forever. Stoddard found he didn't really mind, once he had recovered from the loss of face.

If Ben had been an insect, and some people said that he was, he would have been a blend of bee, dung beetle, and spider. He flitted from one feeding place to another, looking not for nectar but for dirt, and when it was gathered, he would spin it out again, not as honey but as a more acidic substance, stringy, and tending to stick to those foolish or unlucky enough to walk into it.

The man had opened every medicine cabinet in Appleboro and knew whose brilliant smile required stickum for his or her false teeth, who was constipated, and who was on tranquilizers. (If the prescription on the pills was too old, then he knew who was off tranquilizers, which could be fashioned into a tidbit of equal interest.) He had lifted the cover on every saucepan in town, and peered into every cupboard, making a note of which Mrs. Richbitch was saving money on her guests by using store brands instead of the big national names and which Mrs. Lahdeedah was trying to impress people with national brands while her husband's income certainly should have called for generics, my dear!

More than one Appleboro high-society hostess had naughtily placed her new bone-china cup and saucer, purchased on a trip to England, in its teakwood display stand in a manner that would permit her to know whether Ben Stoddard had picked it up to peer at the maker's name on the bottom—the pattern slightly skewed to the left, the handle on the cup not quite parallel to the edge of the shelf, or whatever. She would give her visitor ample opportunity to indulge his curiosity during her absences from the room—"More tea? Another slice of cake? I'll only be a minute!" She could then be satisfied that he had been disappointed to find that the china had derived from the workshop of Josiah Wedgewood and not from the automated factory of a Japanese imitator.

As a schoolteacher in a small town where one knew one's neighbors—and could with a little effort know their business, as well—Stoddard was in an ideal position for prying the latest out of the kiddies. Today, however, school had not been productive, so when the last class was dismissed at 3 P.M., teacher took a brisk walk into the hills. Many years of preaching exercise and fresh air to his charges, and he had come to believe it himself. He was a familiar sight walking briskly down the back roads—jogging was undignified—with fists clenched and bony arms pumping back and forth like an old hen responding to some ancient instinct and attempting flight. He tooled down East Mountainside, waved his comically youthful plaid cap at Harriet Lorimer, and then on an impulse turned up the Oostdyk wagon road across the Belding property. He was fond of the old wagon road, possibly because it had figured so juicily in the most delightful contretemps that Appleboro had seen in years or even just about ever!

He reached the Oostdyk land up above, and observed that Carl Van Houten had stopped his building, probably by court order. There were two frames erected, one with partial flooring already in place, and there were several other foundations under excavation. Enough lumber was stacked to put up at least four houses, he estimated, though none had been brought in since his last expedition up the hill. Satisfied, he turned back. When he passed the Belding place, he stopped to get some water from the still-operational outdoor pump, and then on impulse walked around the cottage to peer into the windows. If Belding's boy Billy had come up and had the place cleaned, that would mean Jason was expected back in residence shortly. The place was still thick with dust. And so, Ben was pleased to note, was an object that shouldn't have been there at all, stretched out on the kitchen floor directly next to Belding's not terribly clean garbage pail.

Undignified or not, he half-jogged home in his hurry to pass along this bit of intelligence, looking as if that hen was about to master the principles of flight after all.

22

"I can't tell you how shocked I was," he was explaining cheerfully to Judith Oostdyk within two minutes of entering his door. "I think Jason must be getting senile to let something like that happen. Senile, Alzheimer's, whatever they call it nowadays. I mean, dear, something like that you can't write off as simple forgetfulness, now can you! *Too much!*" he said, emphasizing each word as he uttered it.

"And listen, his boy'll probably be up to open the house any day now. I wish I could have done something, but short of breaking in, I don't know what it could have been. It makes me sick to think of poor Billy Belding walking in on that!" he concluded, ending thusly on an upbeat.

CHAPTER 8

April 13: Hepatica

*B*ILLY AND GEORGIA Belding were motoring up from New York to open Billy's father's house for him before his return from Florida. Billy was doing it because he sincerely liked his old man—love being a word he couldn't face—and also wanted to be in good standing when next he tried to convince his father to sell Carl Van Houten a right-of-way and take the rest of the property at the same time. Georgia was along because she sincerely was bored silly by her father-in-law, but wanted to stay in his good graces for the same reasons that her husband did.

"I think it's selfish of Dad," Georgia announced. "What's he need that old place for, all that land, at his age?" She pouted quite becomingly for a thirty-five-year-old, though the pouting habit was etching lines from her nose to the sides of her mouth. Irritably, she brushed a lock of blond (natural!) hair off her forehead.

Billy shrugged his shoulders and turned briefly toward his wife. "Same reason anybody needs anything: He wants it. Same reason we need a place on the island, a boat." Georgia and Billy didn't fight very often, but they nevertheless instinctively lined up on opposite sides of most issues as a sort of emotional exercise and as an unconscious

24

participation in what they found to be the game plan for a successful marriage: Thrust makes parry makes counterthrust makes synthesis and understanding on a higher level, if you can last that long.

Of course, if they didn't fight, they each still kept score in the event that it ever should be necessary to decide who had managed a technical knockout. If Billy suggested the theater, Georgia happily agreed, but added, "Try not to get tickets so far down front this time; I don't like to look at their tonsils." And if Georgia announced, "I'm going to Saks this afternoon. Want I should pick up a necktie? You could use one," Billy's reaction was, "Thanks, Georgie. Good idea. But let's match my gray pinstripe, not your new bag, all right?"

"When's Dad getting back?" Georgia asked. "You get any mail from him?"

"Didn't write. But sometimes he doesn't. Always here by the last week in April anyway, sprinkles a packet of lettuce seeds out back, buys a couple of tomato seedlings. Don't let me forget to call someone to till the kitchen garden. If the weather stays good, maybe we can check in at Mountain House tonight, go home tomorrow."

"Oh, I don't know. I'd just as soon get it over with and head home."

"Do us both good. Stay overnight, get a little fresh air."

"If you say so," Georgia agreed with passionless boredom. Thrust, parry, counterthrust.

They rode in silence until the Appleboro post office, where Billy stopped to pick up the mail they'd be holding for his father's return. He failed to recognize the clerk. "Hi, I'm Jason Belding's son, William. I've got the key to my dad's box here, but I think you've probably got his mail in a couple of cartons for me to pick up."

"Oh, yes, Mr. Belding. I'm Don Smith, the new postmaster. Glad to meet you, sir."

A clerk in back, happy to score one over the new

25

postmaster, whom she loathed, called out, "Hey, Billy boy, how's it going, kid? World treatin' ya right?"

"Dolly," Billy said, "good to see you! Great! How you?"

"Terrific!" Dolly turned back happily to sorting the mail, satisfied that she had shown the new boss that she was the one who belonged, not him, the fink.

Two cartons of mail deposited in the car, mostly junk from the look of it, and Billy and Georgia were off for East Mountainside Road and the house. Once inside, Billy dumped the cartons on the kitchen table. "Post office'll want the boxes back. Let's get some windows open, hon. Musty in here."

"Musty, hell, it stinks. I'll start in the living room. You take the kitchen."

They started their rounds, pulling up windows, or if the lower part was stuck, pulling down the top half, or if both were jammed, banging on the frame with their fists until one section or another could be made to move. Then Billy called, "Oh, Lord, Georgia, look at what the hell we've got here in the kitchen!"

Georgia joined her husband. "Oh, no, what is it, the cat? How could the old man have left her here like that? Christ! Poor dumb beast must have starved to death." She turned away but recovered sufficiently to remark, "Thanks a bunch for asking me in for a look."

"I don't know how he could have forgotten to board her at a farm until he got back. He'll be miserable about this. Listen, dear, I can't touch the damn thing, so I'm going to look for a shovel or something to pick it up with. You find something I can put it in and I'm going out to the bottom field and bury her." He shook his head. "Poor old Jezebel."

Twenty minutes later, Billy was back, pale and shaken. "How could Dad have done this?" he asked of no one, though Georgia answered.

"I'll tell you how. He's getting senile, that's how. If

he wasn't, he wouldn't have forgotten the cat, and he wouldn't be so blind and stubborn about selling out to this Van Houten."

"I'm worried sick about him."

"Who, Van Houten?"

Billy looked at his wife in disgust. "Yeah," he said sarcastically, "Van Houten."

CHAPTER 9

April 18: Dandelion

*C*ARL VAN HOUTEN, at age thirty-eight, was undoubtedly Appleboro's most successful native son. He had begun, like his father, as a carpenter, moved on to building simple structures and then houses, and finally, discovering a skill for financial dealing equal to the task, had become a developer. His residential developments were highly regarded along the coast from Massachusetts to Florida, and with good reason, though largely by people who didn't live in them—merchants, landowners, bankers with mortgage money to dispense. There were, however, occasional rumblings about too many houses on soil that couldn't support the septic systems adequately, or on roads that were unable to bear the extra traffic. (Van Houten had once been accused of doing a traffic survey on a snow-emergency day, when very few cars were trying to face down the weather, but nothing was ever proved to anyone's satisfaction, including Van Houten's, who claimed he had been maligned, and even threatened suit against his accusers.)

Environmental groups had listlessly (and impotently) insisted that one of his developments in North Carolina was an insensitive disfigurement of the landscape and was inevitably doomed to become a rural slum. Van Houten and his supporters pointed out that his houses may not have been as pretty to look at as God's unspoiled hills, but on the other hand, the unspoiled hills weren't much at giving employment to local workmen, store clerks, garage owners, refrigerator salesmen, schoolteachers, or anybody else.

At the moment, Carl Van Houten was in a small meeting room of the Waldorf addressing a group of potential investors in his latest condominium venture, a venture that to him would be the most important achievement of his professional life. He was going home to Appleboro. He was an inheritor of the Dutch and Huguenot traditions as much as any Oostdyk, but where the Oostdyks had become bankers and landowners, the Van Houtens had labored on the land. Now he would be an equal inheritor, with an equal place in the community. He stood in front of his audience, his eyes still the confident clear blue of an honest country boy, his fair hair, though thinning, still falling into his eyes, looking innocent as a farm lad sitting on a rail and chewing on a piece of straw. Only a slight puffiness to his face and an increasingly obvious need to decide whether to wear his belt above or below his stomach hinted at a more opulent lifestyle than was available to the average youngster from Appleboro.

"I'm sure that what I've had to say to you gentlemen will be of interest," he concluded. "My associates have brochures to pass out, including sketches of the development, financial projections, and federal and state tax consequences. We'll adjourn now for cocktails, and my associate Chris Morton and I will be happy to answer your questions. Jes' don't make 'em too tough."

There was a ripple of laughter and the twenty-odd guests headed for the bar and the hors d'oeuvres selection. Several, after encumbering themselves with plates of canapes, speared shrimp, pickles, and sausages in one hand and a beverage in the other, gathered around. "Isn't that

29

pressing an expensive development a little," one asked, "two hundred homes on two hundred acres?"

Van Houten grinned. "It certainly is. That's very perceptive. You see, these days, whatever you propose, there's gonna be somebody against it. If I submitted plans for a hundred houses, somebody'd be on his feet at the town meeting yapping about the water supply, the rape of the environment, and whatever else is fashionable that week. They'd be calling for no more than fifty home sites. Believe me, I know these longhairs."

"Well, what about the water supply and the environment?"

"Listen." Van Houten poked a finger in his questioner's chest. "The state isn't going to let us build anything the land can't support. That's all been checked out, I assure you. I can give you chapter and verse on how deep the soil is, the drainage rate, the capacity of the aquifer. Anything you want. The point is, I don't *want* to build any two hundred units. After they start howling, we'll voluntarily cut down to a hundred, donate a patch of land to the town for a park, they want it that way, and everybody's happy! You dig? Makes us the good guys in everybody's book, right?"

"Uh," one potential investor said hesitantly, "it sounds like you expect trouble, would you say? I mean, speaking for myself, I don't want to step into a hornet's nest. Who needs it?"

Van Houten smiled and shrugged casually. "Not to worry. Suit yourself, of course. It's your money and none of us is about to try to pressure you. Believe me, it's like this all over, and if you handle it right, it doesn't amount to a hill of beans. It's this way: There'll be some fuss and feathers, but a little town like Appleboro, it'll be up to the town board. And who do you think is the town board?" he asked with a confidential smile. "I'll tell you. Nobody in his right mind wants a job like that for a couple of thou a year and lots of headaches except the people it really matters to, and that's the big landowners and the folks who want to develop the land. And one or two public-spirited citizens who sometimes make waves a little, but you can forget about them."

His voice rose a little, so everyone in the room could hear. "Now there's some people say these little town boards, they couldn't figure out the cost of seventy-nine one-cent stamps without a calculator. Personally, I resent that. These people are sincere and dedicated, and at least as far as Appleboro goes, I say they could too figure out the cost of seventy-nine one-cent stamps, if it really got to be important."

A little laughter ran through the room and Van Houten continued. "Of course, if they hadda make change from a dollar, maybe it'd be different and they'd have a spot of trouble." The laugh was louder. The staff members of Van Houten Enterprises smiled, but without parting their lips; after all, they had heard the boss's little joke, or an appropriate variant thereof, on many similar occasions.

Van Houten hoisted a glass. "Gentlemen, here's to Mountain Vista Estates. And to those of you who join us, welcome aboard." He sighed appreciatively. "Ah, that's good! Oh, yeah, there's one thing I could add, for what it's worth. I hail from Appleboro myself originally, and I know the place. That's why I want to develop there, do something for the old hometown. It's a good town. People are friendly, neighborly; everybody gets on, looks out for everybody else. When I see some other places, they make me sick the way people go around kicking each other on the tail. But not Appleboro; only the devil would get sick in Appleboro; not enough business for the old boy." He laughed again, rattled the ice in his glass, and tilted it to drain the dregs.

31

CHAPTER 10

April 20: Spring Beauty

"**M**R. BELDING," THE smoothly professional voice cooed, "I appreciate your concern, but like as not, there's nothing to worry about. Your father reserved his usual studio apartment at a very nice little building we've got just north of Lauderdale, but then, as I've told you, he never showed up."

"Yes, but that's not like him. He's never done anything like that before."

"I understand. But people get a little older," the buttery tones went on, "sometimes they take strange ways. Last year one of our regulars ran into a friend, went to St. Pete, and never thought to cancel with us. You know? I'm sorry I can't help you. Maybe you wait a bit longer, he'll turn up. If he doesn't, then's the time to get in touch with the authorities. Good luck, Mr. Belding. I'm sure it'll all work out."

Billy knew when he was being dismissed. "Thanks." He hung up. He strode into the kitchen, where Georgia had been listening on the extension phone. "You hear that, hon? What do you think?"

Georgia continued to discipline an incipient hangnail as she answered. "I don't know, dear," she said, disassociating herself from the problem. "Maybe they're right. Why don't you call Harriet Lorimer and talk it over with her first?" she added, taking the burden off Billy's back, as well; she was feeling generous.

"I wish you wouldn't do your nails at the kitchen table."

"Why ever not?"

"Because it's— Just because." He ran his fingers through his hair nervously. "Oh, hell, forget I said it, okay? I'll call Aunt Harriet. Maybe I'll drive up there."

"Whatever you think best." Georgia frowned at her left thumbnail and told herself, not for the first time, that she simply had to stop gnawing away like a nervous schoolgirl; that uneven edge was unbecoming, to put it mildly.

Billy spun around and strode out toward the other phone. He dialed Harriet. An operator came on and informed him that the number he was calling was temporarily out of service. That meant it had been raining hard in Appleboro; whenever it rained hard in Appleboro, the phone gave up in some sort of existential despair. Why didn't they just say it was shot to hell, instead of all this temporarily out of service bull, damn it!

Harriet was on the terrace enjoying the fresh, clear air after the storm had passed. She shook her head vigorously, in tune with the breeze that was dancing through the live gray hair she knew she was too proud of. Lord, but I love it when it's like this, she thought, and she noted that in the temporarily clean and sparkling world that stretched down the hill, even the garbage in Jason's field had stopped rotting; at least the birds had given up circling and swooping.

At times like this, she told herself, I'm ready to be young again. Or at least I would be if the phone would start working for a change; I want to talk to somebody besides myself. As if by magic, a figure appeared, trudging sadly along East Mountainside, doing the things a timidly defiant

33

child is wont to do, such as scuffing its shoes and stepping in puddles: Melvin Spingle. "Hey, Melvin," Harriet screeched like one of the boy's contemporaries, "c'mon up! Cookie, cookie! C'mon!"

The boy climbed the hill and wheezed like the un-athletic child he was. "Hi, Mrs. Lorimer," he said in muted tragic tones.

"All right, Melvin, what is it? What's wrong?"

"Nuthin'," the martyr replied, hoping to be asked to explain.

"Okay, boy, out with it. No story, no cookie," she said firmly, figuring that the child was generations too young to understand "No tickee, no shirtee."

"Nobody believes me none of the time, Mrs. Lorimer. I told them how I seen this spooky skeleton that got killed and maybe even slain, even. So then my pa yells, and the cops say how I should see this doctor for crazy people. But I seen it, honest I did." He looked at her, half-pleading, half-resentful.

"*Saw* it, Melvin."

"Okay, saw it. But I did. You don't believe me, either."

It was true, but having done time helping one generation of children face reality, Harriet felt inadequate to taking on the task a second time. "'Course I do, Melvin. If you say you saw it, you saw it. Now how about a Coke and cookie?"

"Yeah. Thanks, Mrs. Lorimer." The boy consumed the goodies in tragic silence, wallowing in his martyrdom, though as a decent sort of saint, he took sufficient time out to mumble, "It's good, Mrs. Lorimer. Thanks a lot. I gotta go home now."

Harriet sent him on his way and smiled as she watched his dignified descent down the driveway. She prepared to go in, and as she took a last look down the valley, the bright blue garbage caught her eye again. She hesitated and frowned. "No way," she said aloud. "Cut it out, girlie.

34

You're alone too damn much; that's your trouble." She opened the screen door to go in, and as she did so, she added, "Jason, where the hell are you? Get your ass back onto East Mountainside so I can kick it back off again, you hear me?"

As she shut the front door, she glanced at herself in the pier glass her husband had put up years ago so she could check her appearance on the way out for the evening, and later on to see how she had survived the festivities when they came back through the front door. She ran her hands appraisingly down her ample front, brought them to rest on her pelvis, and cocked her head saucily in a way that had slain the boys in high school over forty years ago. She caught her own eyes in the reflection and spoke aloud again. "Oh, for God's sake, come off it, you batty old crock."

With a deep sigh, she headed for the kitchen and the single martini she allowed herself of an evening, fully aware of the extent to which she was enjoying a greedy portion of self-pity.

The phone rang. Delighted that it was working again, she told herself that it had to be Jason calling at last. "Hello?"

A young woman's voice asked, "May I speak to Harriet Lorimer, please?"

"Speaking."

"Oh, hi, Harriet. How are you this beautiful day?"

"Fine," Harriet replied, suspicious of being jock-eyed into friendly terms with a voice she wasn't sure she recognized. "How're you?"

"Just great! Listen, Harriet, I'm calling from Poughkeepsie Everlast, and I want to tell you about the special offer we've got for you on our top-grade vinyl siding. Do you own your own home?"

Rage boiled up the way a pot of spaghetti goes wild when the flame is turned too high and the cover is on too tight. "Young woman," Harriet said, trying to simmer down, "I don't consider myself on a first-name basis with strangers clearly half my age or less. Furthermore, I don't pay for a telephone for people to intrude with sales pitches. It's not your fault; you're only trying to make a buck, calling when your boss says so, but—" Her voice was getting higher, and hoping (erroneously) that she was cutting this off before the caller realized how close she was to tears, she yelled, "Oh, shove your damned top-grade vinyl siding!" and slammed down the phone.

Pouring her martini, for which she had lost her taste, down the drain, Harriet went upstairs to lie down, a wad of tissue in her hand for eye dabbing. The phone rang. Why did I ever want it back in working order? she asked herself. It stopped after at least a dozen rings.

Ten minutes later, it started up again. With an exasperated sigh, she picked it up. It was Billy Belding. "Oh, Billy, no!" she exclaimed after the boy had told his story. He went on with the rest of it. "Of course you should! You come up here and I'll go with you. We'll see Bob Pettit in the morning."

Afterward, she went down and ate some salad left over from lunch, too dispirited to try cooking. "Jason," she said again, softly, "come on back and I won't kick your ass off East Mountainside. I'll nail it in place instead. Okay?" she pleaded.

CHAPTER 11

April 20: Rue Anemone

CARL VAN HOUTEN sat in his second-story office and looked out on Appleboro's Main Street. He disapproved of what he saw, the shabby late-Victorian buildings, the pitiful stabs at elegance of elaborate cornices and intricate stonework around the windows and doors, but he liked seeing it: It was ripe for redevelopment. He poked a paper clip in his ear and wiggled it about, prospecting for wax. He didn't need an office in Appleboro, but he had taken it anyway, as a rare sentimental gesture. He had come home. He wished his daddy could have seen this. The same weekly newspaper that had carried Pa's handyman ads ("No job too big or small. Call after 5 and ask for Alec.") would soon be sporting full-page layouts for Van Houten Enterprises, inviting the public to "let us show you the house of your dreams."

Besides, sentimental gesture or not, he had bought the building, and once Mountain Vista Estates was finished, he intended to turn it over at a handsome profit and move on to someplace that mattered.

Which reminded him: "Hey, Chris," he bellowed into the outer office, "shake a leg with that report, will you? What's in it? Whatta they got to say? We haven't got all day."

Chris Morton sighed. At investors meetings, he was an "associate," whatever the hell that was, but back in the office, he was a fancy office boy when the old man was in a good mood, and a whipping boy when he wasn't, which was now. He gathered up the computerized analysis the trendy firm of accountants they were using had submitted, comparing the profit potential of building on Oostdyk's land, where the houses with their attractive mountain views would bring top dollar, with building on Jessup's less desirable land, where the deal could go ahead without delay but where the houses would bring in less. Various assumptions were made: It would take three to six months to get the access road through Belding's land taken care of; it would take six months to a year; it would take longer. The buyers of homes on the Oostdyk land would be less affected by downturns in the economy than those who would spring for the less expensive plots on the Jessup land, but they'd be more demanding in what they'd expect to get. Jessup buyers would have greater delays in getting mortgages. If the Jessup land was developed, what were the options for recouping any of the investment already made on the Oostdyk site? Taking every combination of assumptions, how much less should Van Houten Enterprises pay Jessup in order to realize at least as good a profit potential as with the original plan to go ahead with Oostdyk? And so forth.

Morton felt the perspiration break out on his forehead. His shirt was damp, as well. Morton sweated a lot, and Van Houten knew it, and Morton knew that Van Houten knew it. And that Van Houten liked it that way. How in hell could he give the man a two-minute summary of this gibberish? And, of course, Van Houten would never admit that his fancy accounting firm was a waste of money; he'd find a way to shift the blame to Morton for an inability to keep up with the times, to understand computerized analyses, to summarize them for the man who paid his salary. Morton sighed. Maybe he'd take off for Florida and sell homesites to retired couples from New York grateful for anything that wasn't underwater as long as it was warm enough to keep their elderly bones from aching.

He went in. This time, to his delight, Van Houten's simple faith in the incompetence of anyone he might be paying a salary to worked in his favor. The boss grabbed the report out of his hands. "Lemme see myself." He skimmed the material quickly, punctuating his reading with grunts of understanding, approval, disgust, disbelief, and an occasional "bullshit."

After five minutes of tongue clicking and snorting, he slammed the pages down and looked at his subordinate. "In other words, what these fuckers are saying is that they don't know. Bastards bleed a man dry and give him a stack of paper for his money. That's supposed to make him happy. My own goddamn fault. I ought to know by now I know my business better than these Harvard Business School smartasses. Listen, go down to the deli and get me an antipasto hero. And two slices of pickle on the side. They give you any lip, tell 'em it's for Carl Van Houten. Go ahead now." He turned away and lifted the phone.

Morton went out, an office boy on an errand. He knew they'd be charging an extra quarter for that second pickle and that he'd pay for it himself. And Van Houten knew it, and knew as well that Morton'd shut up about it rather than face the scorn that would be certain to follow. And that, too, was the way Van Houten liked it. Some people were lion tamers; some were mouse tamers. Van Houten was the latter, and he, Morton, was the mouse.

Van Houten put the phone down, having set up an appointment with Jessup. He smiled to himself; the old boy was so eager to load his land onto somebody else that he'd agreed to meet right away, and the devil take what he ought to be doing around the farm. Even offered to come to the Main Street office. These people, he thought. Someone should teach the poor dummies not to look so ready. They ought to make a guy work for a deal. This way took all the fun out of it.

Well, he thought as he drove out, fun be damned, because he was going to shave about 15 percent off Jessup's asking price, the old boy was that hot to sell out. It was a sure thing he needed the money. Van Houten shook his head: These stubborn old fools, bankrupting themselves to keep on farming when the land they were working was worth a mint as simple real estate. Like doing nothing with a gold mine except grow petunias on top. He smiled again; that was good, petunias on top of a gold mine. He'd use that line again later.

He settled back in the Mercedes and let the tape deck blast out. It was turning into a hot day, but he could make it hotter for some than for others. And he would. After he got Jessup's price down, he'd see Oostdyk again and tell him he was backing out of the deal; he couldn't wait any longer for a right-of-way over Belding's land to be produced. Of course, if Oostdyk wanted to renegotiate at a lower price, he'd think about it. But time is money, right?

He smiled for a third time. The Oostdyk property was his preference, but if he could play these rubes against each other, what the hell. It was going to be a good day, he thought as he sprang youthfully out of the car in front of the Jessup place; and if he could have jumped out of his body and kissed himself full on the lips in awe and admiration, he would have done so, though he would have denied any such thoughts.

"Morning, Mr. Jessup, Mrs. Jessup!" he said once inside. "Beautiful day."

"Nice enough," Til Jessup said as her husband nodded.

"Well, it's good to see you. I used to pass by here on my way to school when I was a kid. Always liked looking at this place. And any day you see an old friend's a beautiful day, right?"

Art Jessup didn't understand small talk and contented himself with looking miserable. His wife nodded curtly. "Coffee, Mr. Van Houten?" she asked.

"Why, I'd like that. And call me Carl, please. May I call you Til? Art?"

"No," Til said, "I don't think so. You're too much younger, you are."

Van Houten laughed. "Right you are, Mrs. Jessup," he said heartily, "right you are."

Til Jessup left the menfolk to their conversation while she busied herself with the coffee. A woman's place, she knew, was to make herself scarce while the business talk was going on, but she listened carefully. This loudmouth was cutting down his offer to Art. And he had never liked looking at the place the way he said. What he liked was throwing stones at the chickens, and sometimes he'd hit them, too. Once she had seen him grab a baby chick and—but she'd try not to hold these cruel pranks of childhood against him. Not for her to judge, even if he had been a bad influence on Bobby. That, in due time, was the work of the Lord. "'God judgeth the righteous, and God is angry with the wicked every day,'" she murmured softly. "'His mischief shall return upon his own head, and his violent dealing shall come down upon his own pate.'"

She went back with the coffee and served. Van Houten, she shrewdly noted, was looking at the cracked china the same way he had taken in the shabby furnishings when he had entered the room. People thought she was simple and they treated her like a child, but there were things she saw, things she knew. One thing she knew was that this man was going to cheat her out of what she and Art had built over a lifetime, and another thing was that if they didn't get the money that was due them, Bobby wouldn't be coming home. Or they wouldn't be going to see Bobby. It wasn't clear which, but it was one or the other. These were things she knew, the way she knew that the Lord would provide. "'I will lift up mine eyes unto the hills, whence cometh my help.'"

"But Mr. Van Houten," Art was protesting, "I'm interested in selling so we can get a little retirement place somewhere, maybe Florida, someplace we can be comfortable, the missus and me."

"—and Bobby," Til interjected.

"And what you're offering, it won't do that. It'd pay off what we owe and that's about it. Leaves us nowhere, not even with a roof over our heads."

"Well, now," Van Houten said, "maybe I can sweeten it a little, but it's not all that bad, is it? You'd still have something free and clear. Maybe you could get a nice studio apartment; a place like that is less work for the lady of the house, and the two of you could be snug as a bug in a rug." He laughed warmly.

Jessup shook his head sadly. "I just don't know."

"Okay, you take your time and think about it. You understand, though, that Henry Oostdyk has lowered his asking price, and what the heck, his place has these mountain and valley views, and it's just plain worth more to me for a housing development. I want to do right by you, but I've got my obligations, too, to my investors and to the people who work for me. Not to mention my own family. So let's say I call you in a couple of days?"

He left, satisfied that he had done a good day's work. The old boy would come down. Meantime, he'd see Oostdyk and put the squeeze on him, tell him that Jessup had lowered his asking price. It was only fair; if a guy made an old farmer squirm, might as well do as much for a soft, fat banker.

In the timeworn parlor, Art Jessup gathered up the coffee things to take back to the kitchen. "What do you think, Til? Should we go along?"

"He was looking at the cookies, I could tell. He was thinking they was store-bought, not homemade like in the old days. He was looking down at us. I could tell."

42

"Oh, Til, Til. I don't know what to do. I don't know anything anymore."

"And we get squinched into Mr. High and Mighty's fancy studio apartment, there'd be no room for Bobby. But he's not going to get away with it. He can't take that Henry Oostdyk land. It isn't right. He's got to take our place, and at a fair price. I tell you that, Art Jessup." She started rocking in her chair and Art saw that her eyes had taken on that blank look again. "'For he shall be tormented with fire and brimstone in the presence of the holy angels, and in the presence of the Lamb.'"

"Please, Til, no more."

"'And the smoke of their torment ascendeth up for ever and ever: and they have no rest day nor night, who worship the beast and his image.'"

Art Jessup knew it was sacrilegious, but sometimes he could get to hate the Good Book, just hate it.

CHAPTER 12

April 20: Marsh Marigold

BACK IN NEW York, Billy Belding had been sleepless. At five o'clock, he finally got out of bed. "Don't you get up," he said to Georgia. "I can't sleep. I'll drive up to Dad's place and as soon as the station house opens, I'll get hold of Bob Pettit."

"What time is it?" Georgia lifted her head and peered at the clock radio. "Oh, Bill, you'll get there years before the station opens. Why don't you relax?" She yawned.

"I can't."

"Oh. Well, okay, but don't do anything foolish."

"Like what? What's that supposed to mean?"

"What's what supposed to mean?"

"Look, you just said— Skip it. I'm on edge. I'll get dressed and be off."

Georgia snuggled down. "Drive carefully," she mumbled.

Billy was at his father's house before eight, too early to call Harriet, too early to call the town police station, an institution that accepted as ordained the thesis that nothing requiring immediate attention could possibly occur between the hours of 10 P.M. and 9 A.M. (And nothing ever had; Appleboro lawbreakers were typically home and watching television by 10 P.M.) He sat in the house he had done so much of his growing up in, moving restlessly from one chair to another, snapping the radio on and off, switching from one television channel to the next without really waiting to see what was being televised. He inspected the bookshelf for its titles, the same bookshelf he had inspected a thousand times before. He considered making coffee but drank water instead.

He went out for a walk, following the same paths he had followed as a boy, and probably kicking the same stones and snapping twigs off the same trees. He walked himself to the point of exhaustion, but nevertheless ran home, getting in the door just after nine. But he forgot about calling Harriet, forgot about the police. Billy Belding had a higher priority; the rest could wait.

The third time he dialed, the phone was finally answered. "Carl, Carl, for Chrissake, where the hell have you been!"

"Who's this?"

"It's me. Bill Belding."

"Christ, it's only ten after nine. Whatta you want, blood? What's up, kid?"

"Listen to me, Carl. Have you got a tarpaulin, something you maybe use around a construction site, cover up the wood or something?"

"What do you mean? Sure I got tarps. So what?"

"Carl, can you get one up to my dad's place? Right away? Just you. No workmen."

"Cut the crap, fellow. What's up?"

"I can't tell you on the phone, damn it!" Billy's voice got as high and scratchy as a crow's. "But you want to get this right-of-way over Dad's land settled, or you want to screw around for another six months? Look, do what I ask and you can start putting up that slum of yours back of this place tomorrow, for God's sake. Just get out here with

45

a tarpaulin and don't ask questions and—Damn! Will you listen to me, Van Houten! You'll see when you get here." He knew he was getting hysterical but he also knew that laying it on as thick as he could was the best way of getting to this slimeball Van Houten; you want to catch an insect, use something sticky.

Van Houten kept a deliberate silence for a good ten seconds and then he said, "Okay, I'll be out. Give me half an hour. It's a pleasure to do business with you," he added sarcastically. "I like a man knows his own mind." He hung up.

Harriet Lorimer had been sleepless, impatient for morning to arrive and with it Billy Belding. She rehearsed over and over the words they would use to stir the local police into action, to get something going so that they could find Jason. She thought of going out to the herb garden to see whether there was any parsley worth cutting yet, but decided against it; suppose Billy phoned instead of coming over and she missed his call that way? The devil with the parsley. Oh, when will that Billy ever show up?

And she, too, paced the floor, realigning vases, sweeping a dead fly off a windowsill into an ashtray (that was all that ashtrays were used for in this house since her pipe-smoking husband's cancer had carried him off), and checking the next day's shopping list half a dozen times. She called Jason's house to get Billy, but this was after he had left the place with Carl Van Houten and his tarpaulin. She considered calling Billy's home in New York, but if he had already left, she might upset Georgia unnecessarily; besides, she didn't need any of that girl's lip right now.

At noon, she decided that there was nothing she could do by staying home except go stark-raving mad, and that the only sensible course was to keep her bridge date at Judith Oostdyk's, bearing in mind to murder that miserable Billy Belding at some later date. The bridge game at Judith's was by way of becoming an Appleboro institution, featuring Harriet Lorimer, Judith Oostdyk, Elfrida Von Hesse, and Jason Belding. During the months that Jason was in Florida each year, Ben Stoddard, the only other available single male of sufficient social standing to be allowed front-door entry into the Oostdyk castle, was accepted as a sorry but manageable substitute, like margarine for butter.

The game had its ritual aspects, and in this sense the current session was no different from any other in the long-standing series. Losers were permitted to exclaim, "I've never had such an awful run of cards," while winners were permitted no more than an inscrutable smile without vocal accompaniment. Criticism was acceptable only to a point: "I think if you had held back the ace and finessed with the queen, you might have made your point," was considered gentle enough, but "I don't see how you can justify a three-spades bid, not with that hand," was forbidden territory, especially since it was sure to be followed by a defensive "I certainly didn't expect you'd leave me with it, partner."

So the game was mannerly enough and the acid was reserved for other, more rewarding batteries. Stoddard began the festivities at snacktime, during creamed mushrooms on toast points. "Ooh," he said, "I love creamed mushrooms. And these are just perfect, Judy, dear. And such a good buy at the Grand Union this week!" A deft thrust cloaked as a compliment: The unwritten laws of Appleboro society specifically barred the upper crust from purchasing fresh produce or meat at a supermarket, especially when they were on sale and were therefore bound to be, as everybody knew, just a wee bit over the hill.

"I'm glad you're enjoying it," Judith said blandly and with creditable understatement as she watched the man eating. Ben Stoddard was scandalously famous for a metabolism as efficient as an automated Japanese factory when directed at absorbing fodder and breaking it into its component nutrients, fibers, and waste before growling fiercely for more. He was, in fact, the perfect guest if you weren't interested in leftovers.

Ben, dispensing with further subtlety since nobody seemed to be getting the point, added, "Yes, good taste doesn't really take a lot of money, I always say." He had heard, and had seen likely evidence, that the Oostdyks were not in the position to live and entertain as lavishly as they once had.

"I agree," Harriet said. "These are delicious, Judy. You must have gotten them from your in-laws' caves up in Saugerties. This never came from a supermarket." The two ladies smiled at each other in happy conspiracy. "I'm surprised you didn't realize that, Ben, and you such a gourmet."

"They're really awfully good," Elfrida Von Hesse said weakly, wishing the trumpet's blare was a bit more distant. Nobody heard her. When fuses are being lit, who attends the buzzing of a gnat? Besides, the woman held herself so rigid, especially in an uncomfortable situation, that an impartial observer might have been excused for wondering if there were times when rigor mortis could set in before death.

Not that Judith Oostdyk and Harriet Lorimer held each other in particularly warm regard. They had little in common beyond one unfortunate aspect of Appleboro life that made an alliance between the two both natural and inevitable, and that was that both Judith and Harriet were dominant women—some would say that dominating was a more precise description of the former—in a world where the role of women had been carved in stone in the early 1900s. Women chose the slipcovers but their husbands set the budget. Menus were determined by the lady of the house so long as the menfolk got their daily beef and potatoes. Women headed charity drives but kept their pretty noses out of government and business, unless it was concerned with the schools.

Both women smarted under the arrangement but

neither was entirely conscious of what it was they were in rebellion against. What they were aware of, however, was that twits like Ben Stoddard were to be kept in line as moral and mental inferiors, whether they wore pants or panties.

Ben retreated in disarray. "That must be it." He laughed. "I should have known better." He opted for a temporary truce, the better to probe the enemy lines at leisure for a more profitable attack point.

As they reassembled after eating, Elfrida, always under the unfortunate delusion that babbling would blow clouds away, trilled, "You'll never guess who was in the library today, just before I closed at noon." Nobody tried guessing. "Jason Belding's boy Billy! I haven't seen him in there in ten years, for pity's sake!" She patted her dull brown hair in place as if readying herself to pose for a picture with a prize swordfish.

Harriet exploded. "Billy! Is he in town? The fool boy was supposed to call me. What did he want in the library?"

"A book, dear," Ben suggested, still resenting Harriet's lining up with the aristos. "What else do people want in a library?"

"Oh, stop it, Ben," Elfrida scolded. "Don't be so smart. What he was after was a law book, of all things. He wanted to look up the Enoch Arden law."

Ben smelled blood. "Enoch Arden? Isn't that the one about people who disappear and never turn up again?"

"I think so, but I don't have law books in my little library. I think it's something about how long you have to wait until they can be declared legally dead. Along those lines, anyway."

An involuntary shudder went through Harriet: How could Jason's boy have been so cold and calculating! Not yet, anyway. "Oh, enough of this. Let's get back to the game."

They did, and they played with only one more interruption, when the younger Oostdyk girl, Sally, a senior at the state university, walked through. "Hi, everybody," she said. "Hey, Mother, if Eddie Baumgarten calls, tell him I couldn't wait. I'll see him at the student union."

"Yes, dear." Judith sighed.

"Don't be so sad, Ma. Eddie's the one you liked. I think."

"Don't be so sure, child. I never form opinions of your boyfriends. By the time I'd come to a conclusion about the current favorite, said conclusion would already be irrelevant, as Daddy's lawyers like to put it." She smiled, but more out of satisfaction with her own wit than from feeling toward her daughter.

"Ha ha, joke. Nice to see you all." The girl left, slamming the front door with a quarter of a decibel more noise than necessary.

"You'll have to excuse her," Judith said perfunctorily. "She's at that age."

"Of course," Harriet said.

Elfrida made concurring noises.

"Pity," Ben said happily, "she isn't going through Vassar like her sister and you did, Judy. Baumgartner. Sounds like one of these kids comes up from New York to get into the state university. Nicer class kid in Vassar." Translation: You need big bucks for Vassar.

"It doesn't matter all that much," Harriet protested. "After all, Ben, you went to a Methodist college in South Carolilna, didn't you? Didn't do you any harm. You even met your wife there, if I'm remembering correctly." Again, she and Judith smirked cheerfully at each other. "And I think the name was Baumgarten."

"Oh, certainly, certainly. I didn't mean anything special. Just an observation, dear," Ben said, once again in retreat.

At the end of the session, the two visiting ladies retired singly to the bathroom, while, as was only proper, the male visitor waited for his turn. Once inside and with the door locked, he muttered, "Bitches," softly, and proceeded to examine the contents of the room for his own particular fun and profit. First, there was the cake of green soap, Palmolive, he thought, where Judith used to have those little balls of scented soap, carved like flowers, in a variety of colors. And leftover slivers of some white variety—Lux? Ivory?—pressed into the green cake. Tacky, tacky. He, Ben, would never stoop to such economies, and he had to get by on a schoolteacher's salary.

He turned next to the medicine cabinet and peered inside at its treasures. A bottle of painkiller, left over from Henry's operation last year, to judge by the date on the prescription label. A rather largish new prescription for a tranquilizer to be taken "three times a day or as needed." Somebody was awfully nervous. He saw the usual hemorrhoid nostrums, the denture cleanser, the depilatory, each of them material for a fun story, but nothing really new and different. Sadly, he began to close the cabinet door when his eye was caught by something dark gleaming through the amber plastic of a prescription vial. He withdrew the vial from its shelf and looked inside. It was strange, he thought, and he wasn't sure what to make of it, though he knew that sooner or later he would be making something of it.

Harriet's voice boomed through the door. "Ben! If you're finished with the inventory of Judith's goodies, Elfie says she'll walk you partway home."

Ben heard the speaker and his hostess laugh, but not Elfrida; her ladylike gasp of dismay wouldn't have carried all that well. And she'd never have yelled in at a fellow like that, either. "Coming," he called back, as he hastily shoved the bottle back in the cabinet and exited.

Walking home with Elfrida, Ben asked, "Elfie, do you have any books on gemstones in your library?"

"Not very much. We're such a tiny operation. We've got a few picture books, though, and I can get something else for you through an interlibrary loan. What is it you want to know about?"

"Oh, it's not important. Just something I'd like to look up."

But Elfrida Von Hesse was not such a fool as she knew the town thought her to be. Ben Stoddard was up to his usual mischief; she could sense it. Her own people had come over as part of the Hessian contingent that had fought in the Revolution, and deep inside that mousy superstructure lurked a stubborn German soul prepared to be as aggressive as the occasion required. "Well," she said sharply, "if it's not important, it's not important. But you're free to come in any time you like. The library's open to all." She hoped he wouldn't come in.

Ben looked at her in surprise. There she was again, ramrod straight, her shoulders hunched, bristling like a porcupine. You never knew with Elfie Von Hesse. Faded into the woodwork most of the time, but every now and again she'd take notions. He decided to make a peace offering. "Say, listen, dear, but did you hear about Judith's brother's wife, if that's not too complicated? Anyway, it seems the Janviers were up to Provincetown, and he decided that she was getting too chummy with some coast-guardsman in a restaurant, which if she had any sense she probably would have been, and anyway he was probably loaded as per usual, so he jumped up from the table in the P-town Inn with a glass of perfectly good wine in his hand and without a word he—"

"No," the little librarian snapped, "I didn't hear of it, and I don't want to hear of it, either. Really, Ben, no matter what these people do, and I know a lot of them act like damned fools, they're still entitled to a little consideration. So, no more, please." What she meant was that Bertie Janvier was Old Appleboro, whether he jumped up from a table with a glass of wine or slid under it with a bottle of rum. "And this is where I turn. I'll see you soon."

Elfie continued down East Chestnut and as she looked at her town fondly, her bristling subsided. She knew the history of every house and every family that counted, and the ones that counted were those whose people had come over even earlier than hers. She understood their heritage better than most of them did themselves, and she looked on them almost as the children she had never had, children who had to be taught and watched over. And sometimes disciplined.

Judith Oostdyk was straightening the house after her guests had departed. No ashtrays to empty these days, thank goodness, since so few people smoked. She rinsed the dishes off and put them in the dishwasher, noting that it would be full enough after dinner tonight to do a load. Or, if she washed a couple of plates now, it could wait until morning and the weekly girl would take the whole thing off her hands.

    The afternoon had left her with a headache. Ben Stoddard had been so sweetly nasty, the way he could be sometimes. He was amusing, there was no one more eligible available, but the man was such a sneak. No wonder his wife had skedaddled. She went to look for an aspirin. One of Henry's medicines, which were always on the top shelf of the cabinet, had been moved down a shelf. She shook her head in mock disbelief and smiled: Ben Stoddard again. She would straighten the place up tomorrow, she decided. Right now she was tired and would have a lovely lie-down until Henry got home.

CHAPTER 13

April 20–21: Jack-in-the-Pulpit

WHEN HARRIET GOT home after the bridge game, she found Billy Belding waiting for her on the patio. "Where in heaven's name have you been?" she started.

Billy cut her short. "I couldn't wait, Aunt Harriet. I went right to the station and told them about Dad. By the time I was through, you must have been out. I tried to reach you a dozen times."

"What's Pettit going to do?"

Belding shrugged. "I don't know what they do. 'Set the wheels in motion,' he keeps saying. How's a small-town cop know what to do, anyway? Look, I've got to go home tonight. I can't stay away from the office, and Bob said they'd keep in touch with me. I filed papers with them, some fool papers about Dad. I don't know . . ." He trailed off. "I just don't know."

"I'll keep after them," Harriet promised, slipping into her old role of a little boy's courtesy aunt. "Don't you worry about that."

When Billy had driven off, Harriet stood silently on the terrace. The sun had sunk behind the cliff, giving East

Mountainside Road its typical early sunset. She peered gloomily over the wall and down the hill into Jason's meadow and saw it even and green and lush. The garbage that had been there for so many months, and even this morning, was gone. It was almost disappointing: There was nothing to complain about. Then a chill struck her, though there was no breeze and the day was warm.

She went inside and called the Spingles and asked whether she could speak to Melvin. "About the school picnic, Dorothy. I want to ask Melvin if he thinks the kids would like the little clearing we've got farther up the hill. You know, screened-in gazebo and everything."

When Melvin got on, Harriet dutifully asked him about the clearing and paid no attention to the response. "Oh, another thing, you know that skeleton you saw and nobody would listen when you told them about it?"

"Yeah. I don't think I should talk about it."

"Just one question, sweetheart. Did it have anything blue with it, maybe something it was wearing or carrying? Something bright blue."

"Oh, it sure did!"

"Oh, that's so nice, Melvin! What was it?"

"It had a, a big blue banner with two dragons on it like knights carry. And, uh, a real big spear with a blue handle and priceless jewels and they was all blue. And—"

"*Were* all blue, dear," Harriet said sadly as she hung up.

Nevertheless, she called Bob Pettit and told him what she wanted.

"Heck, Mrs. Lorimer, we can't start any searches now. Time we got going, it'd be dark. Maybe tomorrow."

"No *maybe*, Bob. Tomorrow. I'll get the Spingle boy if I have to drag him out of school, and you be here without fail."

"Yes, ma'am." These old people, he thought. They took notions. Bad as the Spingle kid. Bob Pettit was twenty-three, young enough to think Harriet old enough to take notions, but also young enough to be unable to resist an order from anyone as old or older than his parents.

The next morning, Harriet charged into action again, on the phone with the station and the Spingles (Dorothy and Melvin both) and back to the station, then once more to the Spingles to arrange for Melvin to be delivered during school-lunch period. I feel, she told herself, as if I was trying to round up a herd of mindless cattle.

At 12:30 the group assembled on the Lorimer patio. There were Harriet, Melvin, Bob Pettit, and, since she was determined to keep her little madman from finding the lost continent of Atlantis in the swamp down the hill and laying claim to it in the name of King Arthur, Dorothy Spingle. They set off and Harriet noted with intermingled satisfaction and fear that Melvin was leading them on a direct course toward the spot where the bright blue garbage had blighted the landscape for so long.

Melvin stopped. "It's around here somewhere, men. And Mother and Mrs. Lorimer. Spread out and deploy the area."

"Oh, hush up, Melvin," Dorothy Spingle said. This is what she had been afraid of. "Speak English and stop playacting. You wouldn't want your father to hear this, would you?"

"Oh, gee. Okay, Ma. We sort of have to look around here."

They looked. They poked into tall clumps of weeds and under fallen saplings. Their shoes squished into wet spots concealed by the spring grasses; their feet got wet. Bob Pettit looked at Harriet, his expression a bastard offspring of triumph and deference, superiority and respect. "Well, Mrs. Lorimer, that's it, I'd say."

Harriet ignored him. "Melvin," she said quietly but firmly, "I want you to tell me the truth about something. No stories. Do you promise?"

Melvin nodded ruefully. "I did see this skeleton. I did. Honest."

"All right, then. Now tell me, when you saw this— When you saw it, did it have anything bright blue with it, and don't give me stories about banners and spears."

"Yes, Mrs. Lorimer." Melvin's voice was tinier than Melvin.

His mother spoke up. "Come along, Melvin. Tell Mrs. Lorimer what you saw." She herself saw the opportunity to demonstrate that her boy was capable of something besides sheer fantasy when the chips were down.

"There was this bag, like the hikers on the mountain have, only not really like what they put on their backs. It was made out of some kind of soft stuff."

"Do you know what canvas is?" Harriet asked.

"Yes, ma'am. It was smoother'n that and I think it had a long strap."

"Thank you, son." Harriet looked triumphantly at Pettit. "Jason Belding has a bright blue flight bag he takes into the fields for picking up rocks or quartz or mushrooms or wild flowers or whatever. He's always doing that. He got it from American Airlines, years ago."

"It said American Airlines on it," Melvin offered hopefully.

The policeman asked, "How come you remember that, boy? I thought maybe you'd be too excited to start reading things like that. Now are you sure it said American Airlines on that bag?"

"No, sir," Melvin said timidly. "I just said that, I guess."

"Thank you, kid." Pettit looked triumphantly at Harriet. "Maybe we better go back up the hill, okay?"

They started climbing back, a search party in defeat. Dorothy Spingle put her arm on her son's shoulder. "Never you mind, dear. You really tried to help, but don't you know we'd love you just as much if you didn't make up these stories?"

Melvin began to sob. So did Harriet, though with less noise. Melvin was crying because he knew he had told the truth, or at least some of what he had told was true, and there was no way he could disentangle fact from fiction and make them understand. Harriet's distress was rooted in her inability to judge whether the failure of the expedition down the hill left her relieved or frustrated; all she could say was that nothing had been accomplished, decided, settled.

That afternoon Carl Van Houten called his biggest potential investor. "Whadda ya say, Joe? Listen, I got some great news. This Appleboro deal is going through even better than we projected. We'll be closing with Belding in a couple days for that right-of-way, and there's a damn good chance we'll be getting his land, too. . . . Yeah, I can practically taste it. Take my word for it. Sure I'm sure. And if that's not enough, I'm getting Oostdyk to take less. Stick with me, baby, and we're in like Flynn. . . . Maybe not exactly like Flynn, but this is even better, right?"

Henry Oostdyk sagged into an easy chair when he got back from the bank that evening. "I think we're almost over it. It's almost finished."

"What's almost finished, Henry? Or were you referring to us?"

"Please, Judy. I'm so tired. The Belding business, of course. It's going to be very soon now. Very soon and we'll be out of the woods."

"Oh, don't tell me! Has Jason finally seen the light? Is it settled at last? Thank God. What's happened?"

Henry looked doubtful; perhaps he shouldn't have spoken. "Ask me no questions," he said, trying without success to be playful, "I'll tell you no lies." He smiled at his wife.

"And if I ask you questions?"

"I'll tell you lies, old puss."

Harriet was too nervous to sit home that evening. The prospect of waiting for the police to follow through on a missing-person report was unbearable, and yet knowing that the wheels were beginning to turn was equally bad; she had spoken of the unspeakable and was thereby forced to face what she dreaded facing. She had summoned up the devil and started a chain of events that she was afraid would only end in disaster.

Though the night was warm, Harriet huddled inside a sweater. The house was laden with gloom despite her turning on every light and trying to concentrate on the fresh flowers in the living room. She felt suffocated, as if just emerged from an air-conditioned theater into a steamy August heat wave so oppressive that it was nearly impossible to breathe. Only now there was an overlay of fear and doubt to make the situation even more intolerable. She had to do something, anything. No, she had to do something for someone, so she took a loaf of bread freshly baked that morning, added a few more comestibles, and headed out for the Jessup place. Til had been one of her favorites before the woman's mind had gone, and Harriet looked in on an irregular basis to see what she could do to give the old couple a few minutes of ease and comfort. It was a mistake.

"She's going on real bad today," Art Jessup explained. "She's got on to Carl Van Houten being why she can't see her boy. Maybe you shouldn't stay, Mrs. Lorimer."

"Oh, let me speak to her a minute. Maybe I can say something, cheer her up a little."

Jessup shook his head. "I don't think so, not when she's like this. Bad as I ever saw. You can try if you like, but I don't think so."

He was right. Til looked at Harriet, and said, "I hope you don't come from that evil man, Carl Van Houten. I've always liked you, Harriet Lorimer, but not if you're a friend of his."

"I've come to see you because I wanted to," Harriet said. "I've brought you some raisin bread, just out of the oven a few hours ago." She held the loaf out. "Here, take it."

59

The woman's eyes turned toward the bread but failed to see it. "'All darkness shall be hid in his secret places,'" she said, "'and a fire not blown shall consume him.'"

Harriet put the bread on the table. "Now, Mrs. Jessup, you've got to think of yourself," she said softly, "and not about Carl Van Houten." I don't know what that means, she said to herself, but it seems the right thing to say. "Leave his punishment to God."

"You're right, Harriet Lorimer. 'Every tree that bringeth not forth good fruit is hewn down, and cast into the fire. Wherefore by their fruits shall ye know them.'"

"I'll have to be running along," Harriet said after ten minutes of failure to penetrate Til Jessup's awareness. "Now you take good care of yourself." She stood and went toward the door after planting a gentle kiss on Til's forehead. She wondered whether the woman even noticed.

"You see how it is," Art Jessup said in a whisper.

"I'm so sorry."

"I never thought I'd get to cursing the Bible. All she does now is spout Scripture. I never knew there was so much talk in the Good Book about fire. I don't think she'll ever run out," he said bitterly.

CHAPTER 14

April 23: Wood Anemone

BOB PETTIT SLAPPED himself on the forehead. "Oh, no!" he groaned.

"Well, it is," said the driver of the town truck that scythed down the roadside growth in Appleboro every few weeks during the season, "so get off your duff, son, and follow me out there. I cut the weeds down and I look in the rearview mirror, and son of a bitch, there it is. Whole goddamn thing's got me off schedule. I tossed a couple of branches over it the ladies on East Mountainside shouldn't piss their bloomers, but that ain't gonna last forever. Let's haul ass, boy. I get home late for dinner again, the wife'll have my hide." He snorted. "She hates it when the franks and beans get overdone. Let's go."

The driver led the way in the town truck and Pettit followed in the police car. Turning off the highway onto East Mountainside, they proceeded slightly under a mile until the truck pulled over at the foot of the Belding land and stopped. "Right here," he said. "There's your baby, under those branches. Hope I didn't disturb nothing by piling up the leaves, but I didn't touch the thing. Okay, Bob, I'm on my way. Have fun."

"Thanks," Pettit said glumly, and he watched the truck start up. "Hey, Maxie," he shouted, "do me a favor and keep quiet about this. It'll all come out soon enough, but I need some time first."

The driver formed a circle with his thumb and index finger and wagged it in assent at the policeman. He ground his gears—it was only a town truck—and drove off.

"Jesus," Pettit muttered to himself as he peered through the pile of branches. He saw a bright blue flight bag lying next to the thing, a United Airlines bag. For a minute his spirits rose. The Lorimer woman had yapped about an American Airlines bag; maybe this is some tramp or something. Then his spirits plummeted back to reality. What he needed was a telephone, but he was damned if he'd traipse over to the Lorimer place; she'd go up like a rocket. Start hooting at him for not believing her, like it was his fault. But old Mrs. Mintz, three houses down, was deaf as a post. He'd bellow until she got the idea and let him use the phone. It was humiliating; bad enough the town gave him a six-year-old Chevy for a police car, but worse that they wouldn't spring for a radio so he wouldn't have to go around like a beggar asking to use some old bat's telephone.

After banging on the door for at least two minutes—he knew the old girl would be home—he finally got in and made her understand what he was after. When he got through to the state police, he was connected to the Bureau of Criminal Investigation and ultimately reached Senior Investigator Morrison.

"Yeah," Morrison said wearily, "well, you stand by it on the road until we get there with a truck. Anybody asks you what's up, tell 'em to ef off."

"Roger," Pettit said. A great load was off him as he shifted the bag of bones onto somebody else's back. He had done good, he figured. He thanked old Mrs. Mintz and left, completely unaware that she had screwed on her new hearing aid for the occasion and was on the horn even before he had reached the bottom of the front steps.

Senior Investigator Hugh Morrison stared glumly at the pictures they had taken before the body—or what remained of it—was removed. Here he was, sixty-three years old, could have taken retirement years ago, but he had hung on, not knowing what else to do. Now, when he didn't need it at all, there was this handful of bones demanding his attention, an impersonal superstructure on which flesh and blood had once been draped to make it something called man.

And what the heap was called when it used to be a man was what they were working on now. Curiosity seekers had materialized all over the road by the time he had arrived at the scene, like flies around a dung heap, and the unhappy local copper had looked as if he'd be willing to lie down next to the remains and seek an equivalent oblivion. Several onlookers had let it be known that an Appleboro resident was missing, and as of this moment, the only dentist in town, a Dr. Merwin Brotz, was checking the teeth against his records.

Morrison burped gently and patted his burgeoning stomach, a dear and faithful friend still shakily under control but nevertheless strongly suspected of plotting to blossom forth and take over. He shook his head sadly. After a lifetime in the Bureau of Criminal Investigation dealing with smashed windows and looted liquor stores, kids who vandalized summer cottages and an occasional stolen car, suddenly he was presented with what, judging from the smashed-in skull, was almost certainly a murder.

Why, he asked himself when he was back at the desk, didn't I get this case a generation ago? Who needs it now? Before Marie died, when she was just over thirty and they were still trying for kids, he would have jumped at the chance, the challenge, as the gung ho top brass called it with ringing insincerity, but not anymore. Dear God, he thought, if only I could have had just a couple of years more of auto thefts. It serves me right, staying on when I could have retired back then. I can't parlay this into a career at my age, and if it gets parlayed into anything at all, it'll be an ulcer.

He ran a hand through thinning gray hair and worked it down his face, rubbing an imposing nose, passing a finger thoughtfully along a full and still-youthful lower lip, and ending with a pleasurable tickle of the beginning stubble on a long, determined chin. He stood. With photos of the site in hand, he walked slowly—rarely did he walk quickly anymore—over to an associate.

"Look at this one, Pinky," he said to a redheaded cop at a nearby desk. "Tell me what you make of it."

"It's a picture," Pinky said. "Very nice. Lotsa grass, lotsa poison ivy. Whatcha want me to say, for Chrissake?"

"It seems to me that if this body had been there long enough so there's nothing left now but bones, the grass wouldn't have grown up so nice and green underneath it. The poison ivy, neither. There ought to be some bare spots. I think those bones were moved."

Pinky took another look. "Yeah. You know, I think you got something."

"Me, too," Morrison said, and thought—But what? "I guess now I drop in on some of the good folk on East Mountainside Road." He put his jacket on and fished for the car keys.

"Have fun," Pinky said absentmindedly, his attention grabbed again by a report on a high school principal caught flashing in a bus terminal two stops down the road from the town he lived in. I don't get it, he thought; maybe he's got a real big one, thinks nobody'd believe it, he doesn't show it off, sort of.

"Merwin Brotz," Harriet said, "you can cut that nonsense out. It's me you're talking to, Harriet Lorimer."

"I realize that, Harriet," the dentist said, "but this is a police matter. I have definite instructions not to talk to anybody until I see the cops. That's all there is to it. And I've got a patient in the chair and I can't hang on the phone any longer."

"Bull. You people love to leave patients with their mouths open, gagging away, while you wander off and file your nails in the next room, so don't give me any of that. You hang up and I'll call right back. And I'll keep calling back."

"You call back and I won't answer. For heaven's sake, Harriet, be reasonable."

"No. This is too important to be reasonable. And you'll answer all right. There isn't a dentist on earth won't answer the phone when it could get him an easy thirty bucks off some sucker with a cavity. I mean it, Merwin."

Brotz thought wearily that if only his practice was a shade bigger, he could afford a nurse to field calls like this. But as it was— "All right, you win. But I've got to go now. Call you back in fifteen minutes." He hung up before Harriet could object, and went in to check his patient. "How does it feel now?" he asked earnestly.

The patient, who had heard the dentist on what was obviously a personal call in the next room, spat out four cotton rolls and removed a kind of a sump pump from his mouth. "Why the hell do you people have to ask damn fool questions when a guy's mouth is stuffed full of old rags and machinery? It feels like hell, if you want to know. I need some codeine or something, and I want to get out of here!"

Dr. Brotz gave his patient a couple of pills and a prescription and sent him on his way. I should have been a horse doctor, he thought sadly; there's money in horses, and no sass. He picked up the phone. "Harriet, listen, I shouldn't be doing this, so you've got to protect me, okay? . . . I'm sorry to say it, but you were right. I'm afraid that's the way it is. . . . Yes, I am. No doubt at all. I've been Jason's dentist for fifteen years and I know his mouth like—well, I know his mouth. . . . Oh, don't cry, Harriet. Listen, I've got to hang up. I've got another patient waiting," he said, untruthfully. Then he called the state trooper station and confessed that he had told Harriet, but only under duress. They had taught him in dental school that the most important rule of dentistry in a world

65

devoted to confrontation with an almost religious intensity was Cover Your Ass; only after that came How to Drill a Hole and Stuff It, 201.

"Merwin told you that? Merwin Brotz?" Harriet asked.

"I don't think you're so surprised, ma'am," Morrison said coldly. He stood on the Lorimer patio while Harriet was in the doorway, neither coming outside nor asking the policeman in. He looked at her impassively.

"That—that—dentist!" she said scornfully, snapping the word like a curse.

"Dr. Brotz said you pressured him, said you'd threatened to interfere with his practice."

"He would. Well, I had every right. Jason Belding was my dearest friend."

"No, ma'am, you had no right. You're meddling in a police investigation. The facts'll be out soon enough, but now we've lost the chance to ask questions before people know why we're asking and what we're trying to find out. So you haven't helped at all in the investigation of your friend's murder. And if you want to help, the best thing you can do is not to meddle."

"No."

"What do you mean, 'no'? Don't you think maybe Mr. Belding's next of kin would have appreciated hearing about this before the news was passed on to outsiders?"

"Again—no. I'm closer than any next of kin." Harriet stepped through the doorway and stood out on the patio. "Sit down," she said, waving the detective into a chair. "I mean 'no.' I'm not going to wring my hands helplessly and wait for a gaggle of hidebound bureaucrats chasing pensions to do something. Don't worry, I have no intention of snooping with a magnifying glass looking for clues, but anything I can do or think of doing, I'll do, and without asking anybody's permission. Is there a law against that?"

"If you persist in that attitude, I'm sure we can find one, Mrs. Lorimer. We pension chasers are experts at that.

66

And about you being closer than kin, how should I take that, lady?" Morrison lifted a cynical eyebrow and cocked his head, trying to look like a hardened TV detective who has seen it all and knows that the truth is even nastier than anything he might imagine.

"Take it any way you damn please, Mr. Senior Investigator. You look like you've decided what it means already, so why ask?"

Morrison's face changed, and surprise, even hurt, replaced the leer. "You're right," he said simply. "I'm sorry. But I'd still like you to explain. If you were close to Jason Belding, there's a good chance you can tell me a lot of things I need to know. Okay?"

Harriet's shoulders came down from their perch of high hauteur, her face showing that she knew his words made good sense but that she would prefer to think they didn't. She wasn't at all sure this was going to be one of her all-time favorite people. "Okay. Well, how can I say it? Jason and his wife and my husband and I were neighbors up here for thirty years, first as weekenders from the city, and then, after retirement, as full-time neighbors. We raised our kids together, and his Billy and my Ed were great friends. Then suddenly there we were, I a widow and he a widower, and we needed each other. Or at least I needed Jason; I needed him very much." She looked at the detective.

"I understand. Please go on."

"Look, I don't know if you can put yourself in my place and imagine yourself alone up here, husband passed on, son grown up and on his own, not enough money to go back to New York City even if I wanted to—which I didn't. You start to dollop out your life in meager little treats. Is it Monday? Oh, goody! I'll get a lobster and boil it up, just for myself, and Tuesday the movie house gives me ten percent off for having lived more than fifty-five years. Then Wednesday there's a bridge game. And so on. The blanks I fill in with the garden, the telephone, needlepoint, reading, television, God knows what. If you don't watch it, a body can get to be like a kid with a bag of jelly beans, counting them one by one, separating the grape from the licorice from the orange, doling out one of this and two of that for today, and a couple of others later on, trying not to worry about what will happen when the bag is empty or when you get sick of jelly beans. It can be pretty damned lonely, believe me."

She continued, almost angrily. "Well, Jason and I saved each other from too much of that. We'd eat together most nights, except when he was in Florida, and we took trips together." She smiled in reminiscence. "Sometimes if the hotel rates were high, we'd book in as Mr. and Mrs., long as there were twin beds. What the hell, what'd it matter? We were both pretty long in the tooth and hardly likely to be overcome by uncontrollable passions. Jason was my dear friend and companion, and he kept me from running my life like a retired librarian, neatening the stacks, centering the ashtrays in the smoking section of the reading room, and going home to a hilarious evening of polishing grandma's silver and the copper pots till they shone like mirrors. The hell with that." She fell silent and her eyes appeared to focus down a long tunnel, dark, empty, and cold, and with not a hint of light at the end.

Morrison broke the silence. "I can understand that," he said softly.

Harriet flared into anger again, almost without intending to. "Can you, Mr. Morrison? Can you?" She turned her head away. "I doubt it," she said bitterly.

"Do you think a policeman's nothing but head, belly, and feet?" he asked quietly.

"No," Harriet replied, "just belly and feet. I never would have thought of head at all. No, wait, I'm sorry. I'm just so upset. I apologize."

"That's all right, ma'am. But I'll step out of line, too, just enough to show you something. Maybe we can get along a little better if I do, and maybe that'll help us find out sooner what happened to your friend. Lady," he said, "I know exactly what you mean. You know why I'm a cop? I'll tell you. Because my wife died. Real young. We didn't have any kids and I just kept going the way I was pointed, like a windup toy. That's all I do. You know what? You're lucky, lady. I go home after work and get my dinner, and along about ten years ago, I started to eat canned spaghetti because boiling the stuff up was too much trouble. Why bother? It's only something to load your gut with so you can get to sleep and get up the next day and start being a cop again. A couple of years more, they'll be making me retire. I'll move into a trailer home somewhere and whatever time I don't spend whittling, I'll probably put in opening cans of spaghetti. So I know. I know. And I want to help, if you'll let me."

Harriet's eyes focused in wonder on the policeman. "I'm sorry," she said. "May I ask you a question?" Morrison nodded. "It's that you don't sound like my idea of a policeman. How'd you pick this for your life? Or is that a snobbish thing to ask?"

"That's all right. I joined the force because my father was a cop down in the city. I did it to support my wife and me while I went to Fordham Law School at the same time. But after she died, I figured enough law school. I joined the state police up here where nothing much goes on and tried to keep about a half-step ahead of dry rot. Or damp rot. Or whatever it is that keeps a fellow two steps ahead of being dead."

They both sat in silence. "Uh, don't get me wrong," Harriet said timidly, "but if you don't mind a cold pasta salad—not canned, and a little ham in it . . . And I've got some chocolate mousse," she added hopefully. "What do you think? Interested? It must be near your quitting time."

"As a cop would say, lady, I don't care whether it's a chocolate moose or a strawberry elephant, I'd love it."

Harriet laughed. "Call me Lady Harriet," she said. As they went inside, the policeman turned to Harriet. "Hey," he said, "please don't get me wrong, Mrs. Lorimer. I shouldn't have spoken out the way I did just now, and I'm sorry. All I can say is that I wanted you to know that I could understand what you mean about losing somebody. Talking about my own affairs isn't regulation, if you know what I mean, but if it'll help clear the air so we can get on better with this investigation— Oh, Lord, I don't know what I'm trying to say."

"You don't? That's strange, because I do. Let's agree we both got a little bit out of line, and for heaven's sake, let's drop it there. And let's eat."

"Good idea. When in doubt, eat, I always say."

Harriet looked at the man's waistline. "Would it be too much to say you must be in doubt an awful lot?" She raised a hand against Morrison's reaction. "I take that back, but I couldn't resist."

The two dropped the conversation there and started getting something on the table. Harriet banged bowls, pans, and utensils in the kitchen and bawled orders at Morrison about the china, silver, and crystal to be set out on the dining table. Her laugh was too loud and her voice too shrill that evening; the eternity of not knowing about Jason and the doubts were ended while the abyss in front was yet to be explored. Somehow this stranger who had so infuriated her by prying into a world she was determined would remain private appeared to comprehend what she was saying and what she was leaving unsaid, and somewhere below the level of consciousness she suspected he might be able to steady her resolve as she turned about and peered into the chasm. It was a funny world, she mused, though not in a particularly funny way.

CHAPTER 15

April 24: Wild Columbine

RURAL AMERICA STILL maintains its basic strength of character, even in these times of crumbling values. Grass-roots breeding will always tell, and it was amazing the way most of those affected by the violent death of Jason Belding were able to express their shock and yet manage to get on with things, to smile through their tears and overcome their grief.

Billy Belding told Virginia, "It's over and it's horrible. They found Dad. There on his own place, not a hundred yards from the house."

"Oh, Lord, Billy. I'm so sorry. What happened?"

"Somebody—his head was bashed in."

Virginia sighed. "How terrible." She asked the appropriate questions about when and how and who, and about a funeral service, and then after ten seconds of respectable silence, which seemed only decent, she said, "Sweetheart, what will happen now? About Dad's place, I mean."

"I guess the usual. I assume Dad's lawyer has the will—I'll ask Harriet Lorimer about that, and there's probate and whatnot. I don't know exactly how it gets handled," he said bitterly, "but where there's an estate involved and money for lawyers, it'll all be taken care of without us ever having to trouble our pretty little heads."

"What I mean is, do you think they'll hold things up for long, that you'll be able to make a deal soon with this Van Houten creep?"

"Like I say, anything can be worked out if you've got money to pay for it. I'll bet this is wound up in a month."

"Just as a hedge, I'll lay five bucks it takes longer."

"You're on. Easiest fin I ever made." He kissed her gently on the nose. There's nothing like death to bring the members of a family close to each other, especially when there's a couple of bucks in it.

"Poor Jason," Judith Oostdyk said. "What an awful thing. I simply can't believe it. What ever could have happened, Henry!"

"Sure, it's awful," her husband said, "but come off it, angel. What you really want to ask is what happens next."

Judith smiled. "True, but that doesn't mean I don't care about Jason. However, dear, since you bring it up yourself, what does happen next?"

"I assume the police will be working on it, and that may take forever, but as far as the right-of-way through Jason's place, well, Billy Belding wants that as much as we do. Shouldn't take any time at all."

"Thank God for small blessings." Judith sighed.

"And not so small. Think about that."

"I know. Henry, do you think we'll have the cash soon enough to take Sally out of the state university and get her into Vassar for the fall semester?"

"Very likely. Don't be too sure she'll want it, though, and if she does go, don't count on too much coming of it."

"Oh, she'll meet a much nicer class of people there,

and I'll be so happy to get her away from those kids in New Paltz. And she'll be happy, too."

"Come on, Judy, face it. You can take the girl out of New Paltz, but you probably can't take New Paltz out of the girl, and you know it." He grinned at his own cleverness.

"Oh, you, you're terrible! I'll make you do penance for that, Henry Oostdyk. We're going to Europe next year, and you're going to the Bayreuth festival, like it or not."

Henry shook his head. "Sorry, sweetheart, but it's not possible. I could no more sit through a Wagnerian opera at my age than I could pitch a no-hitter for the Mets. I may look like twenty-eight years old to you, but deep inside there's a middle-aged prostate that needs to take me to the can every couple of hours. Can you see me pushing my way through those dedicated Wagnerites four times a performance?"

"No excuses. I'll get you those incontinence diapers or whatever they call them. I'm sure there's something fashionable I can pick up at Sears."

They both laughed. Judith got up and walked behind her husband's easy chair. She kissed him on top of his head, directly on the bald spot. "Maybe that'll make the hair grow."

"Or singe off the remains." He pulled his wife down on his lap, no mean feat, and kissed her, but directly on the lips, the first time such an event had occurred in years other than as part of a ceremonial farewell in the morning when Henry set off for the bank or as a hail on his return.

The earth moved, though only because each of the Oostdyks was a touch overweight, especially Judith.

Carl Van Houten was whistling and singing softly at his desk. He had seen an old picture on television with a young Ginger Rogers doing a number in pig Latin. "Eeway are in

73

the oneymay," he crooned, "eeway've got a otlay of at-whay it akestay to etgay a onglay."

Chris Morton heard him in the other office and noted to himself that ouyay may be in the oneymay, but what about eemay? Well, I'll be off for that Florida spot in another month. Only have to take a couple days, fly down there, and let them look me over.

"Hey, Chrissie, boy," Van Houten called from the next room, "how's about you go down pick up an antipasto hero at the deli! Get yourself one, too! Things are looking up, up, up!"

Gee, Morton thought, a regular Santa Claus. And he didn't even say about that extra pickle. Maybe I should get it anyway; he could shove it up his duff. "You're on," he called. "Back in ten minutes." He went down the stairs two at a time, thinking happily that the number of times he'd be running this little errand in the future was rapidly dropping toward zilch.

A few of the local folk weren't quite as ebullient. The Jessups, for instance, were regular party poopers. Art liked to talk to Til, just as if she knew what he was trying to tell her. To be honest, sometimes she did, but to be equally honest, she inevitably forgot it a minute later. "Oh, Til," he said, "with poor Jason Belding gone, nothing'll stop Van Houten from closing on the Oostdyk land. And that's what he wants, no matter how much my price comes down."

"I liked Jason Belding. Carl Van Houten should have let him alone. Did he kill him? He was a wicked child and now he's a wicked man."

"Now, Til, mustn't talk like that. Somebody might hear."

"I'll tell Bobby he's got to stop seeing that fellow. People will be talking about birds of a feather."

"Yes, Til. Now eat your soup before it gets cold."

Til wasn't listening. She put her spoon down. "Art, do you think that Van Houten is keeping Bobby from coming home? Keeping him out late all the time. I've got half a mind to—" Her eyes took on the glaze her husband had learned to fear and, more recently, even to hate. "You've got to get Bobby back to his Bible lessons. Let him remember what the Good Book says. 'Incline not my heart to any evil thing, to practice wicked works with men that work iniquity; and let me not eat of their dainties.'"

"You leave this to the Lord," Art warned. "Let him judge."

Slowly the woman turned her head toward her husband and, though her eyes were still unfocused, she seemed to look at him. "You're right, Arthur. It's not for us to be judge and jury. The Lord Himself will judge, and the Lord has judged. 'God shall cast the fury of his wrath upon him and a fire not blown shall consume him.'" She smiled as if she had announced that her God had let the sun come up on a new day, bright, clear, and full of promise.

"Let's clear up the plates and watch television. There's one of the shows you like tonight," Art said.

"Which one?"

"I forget right now."

"Me too."

Ben Stoddard picked up the phone and dialed. "Elfie, sweet, I know it's past eleven but you don't turn in till midnight and I just couldn't sleep. You don't mind my calling, do you? I'm so darned upset."

"You mean about Jason. No, I don't mind, Ben. It's just too awful."

"Yes, it is. Though it's worse for poor Harriet, I suppose. Jason meant the world to her." He sighed.

"I don't know what she'll do, poor thing."

"No. Me, neither. Of course, sooner or later she'll get over it, and I hope that isn't too callous of me to say. And by the way, guess what?"

Elfie knew the point of the phone call was about to

emerge. Ben would never have called at this hour unless he had a little dirt to dish. "What? I can't guess."

"Well, love, I couldn't sleep and I took a walk down East Mountainside this evening, and you know there was a police car outside Harriet's place at ten-thirty! Now you can't tell me a policeman goes and interviews people at ten-thirty. And anyway, I happen to have noticed that that same car was there earlier in the day, late afternoon!"

"Oh, you're kidding!"

"No, I'm not! And the cop didn't come out until a quarter to eleven!"

And you, Elfie thought, hung around to see whether he came out at all and after he did, you hightailed it home to call me, and I'll bet you haven't even taken your sweater off. "I must say, it looks like Harriet isn't taking too long to get over Jason, is she?"

"We shouldn't be jumping to conclusions, should we?" Ben reproved her lightly.

"No, but it's fun, isn't it!" Elfie giggled, as did Ben.

"So maybe all's going to end well and be well, just the way the poet says. Jason's boy will sell the right-of-way, Henry Oostdyk will sell his land, and everything will be hunky-dory in Appleboro. Except," he added hastily, "for poor old Jason, of course."

Elfie philosophized: "Life must go on."

They paused respectfully. Ben said, "The Oostdyks are coming out of this smelling like a rose, aren't they? I wonder if the police will start thinking that Henry had something to do with this."

Elfie's voice took on a sterner tone, fun being fun, but not where the gentry are concerned. "What do you mean by that?"

"Nothing really, but after all, it's Henry who stands to gain the most from Jason's death, isn't it? And let's face it, those two need the money. I mean even an old Dutch family can get desperate, no?"

"Now you stop that! You know how I hate that kind of talk, and I'm not going to listen to it."

"Don't bark at me, Elfrida Von Hesse! You were perfectly happy to practically accuse Harriet Lorimer of sleeping around, but a little joke about Henry Oostdyk and you take off like a rocket. What is this anyway? The Lorimers may not be Oostdyks but they're just as good, aren't they?"

"Yes, they're just as good," Elfie said frigidly. "I never said they weren't. But you damned well know how I feel, Ben Stoddard."

"No, I don't know how you feel. Or anyway, I don't understand it."

"I'll be happy to tell you again. I have two sweaters to my name. One is lambswool and one is cashmere. They're both equally good; they both keep me warm. But the cashmere is special and deserves a little extra care. As sweaters, there's no difference, but when it comes to what they're made of, the difference is enormous."

"So you're saying to me that a Lorimer and an Oostdyk are equal as human beings, but because the Oostdyks are old settlers, they're a more precious possession. You can throw old Harriet in the washing machine, but Henry you've got to do by hand in the bathroom sink."

"You know perfectly well what I mean, even if you're trying to make it sound ridiculous."

"I'm not trying to make it ridiculous. It *is* ridiculous! In fact, it's a lot of . . . of . . . cowflop!"

They hung up simultaneously, neither with a clear advantage but with both in a rage.

CHAPTER 16

April 25: White Violet

ON MORRISON'S INSTRUCTIONS, Pettit met him at the Belding place promptly at nine the next morning. "We'll go over the place," Morrison said, "but since the son and his wife have been here mucking around with things, I don't think we'll find a damn. Let's go."

"Sure thing, Chief. Uh, what are we looking for?"

Morrison snorted. "I was hoping you'd tell me. Just keep your eyes open, see if anything's out of line. I don't know. What the hell, you're a cop. Case the joint."

Half an hour later, they quit. The house was in order; there was no dirty laundry not tucked into the laundry hamper; the wastepaper basket was empty; there were no old newspapers waiting to be thrown out. The desk calendar was open to December 5, the day the man was supposed to have taken off for Florida. "So what do we know now?" Morrison asked. "Either the guy was neat or he was a slob and his son cleaned the place up. Or the son's a slob and his wife cleaned up. That's about it. No unpaid bills, not a personal letter in the place. Not even a stinking bloodstained knife," he added gloomily.

"You want I should go back to the station?" Pettit asked hopefully.

"Not yet. I want you to knock on every door for half a mile on both sides and chat it up with the neighbors. Who'd he talk to, who'd he like, who liked him and who didn't. Get 'em gossiping. You can tell the folks the man's skull was crushed. They know it already, but say it again. They'll love it, and a hot item like that'd start a bronze hunting dog gabbing. Check with me this afternoon. Oh, yeah, you can skip the Lorimer place; I'll talk to her myself. Okay?"

"Roger." Pettit left.

Morrison phoned Harriet. "I usually drop in unannounced," he said. "See what folks are up to. But I'll make an exception in your case."

"How come? You discriminating against me, Officer?"

"Nah. I already dropped in unannounced on you. The shock value's gone. Be right over."

And he was. The coffee Harriet had put on hadn't finished brewing when he knocked on the door. They settled in the living room and Morrison told Harriet what he had accomplished, which, the way he explained it, came to very little. "December 5 is when he was leaving, isn't that it?"

"That's it. Jason trained himself to be methodical. He said one time while he was still working, he forgot to turn the calendar and thought it was Sunday for three days. First thing he did every morning was flip over to the next page and see what he had on for the day. Well, what do we do now?"

Morrison took due note of that "we," but kept his peace. "What I need from you is a rundown of who didn't like your friend Jason Belding, and who stands to gain or lose. What I want you to do is dish the dirt, Harriet Lorimer. You said you wanted to help, and you can save me a lot of time by opening up and letting it all out."

79

Harriet wriggled down more comfortably in her seat and cleared her throat. "The first part's easy; nobody disliked Jason. But there were plenty of people mad at him and plenty who stood to gain. In fact, we can run through a samovar of coffee before I finish telling you about that."

"Good." He got out a pen and asked for some paper. "I'm taking notes, but don't let that hold you back. Shoot."

Harriet told the detective about the right-of-way that Jason refused to sell and how that made at least three people—Billy Belding, Henry Oostdyk, and Carl Van Houten—"extremely unhappy, to put it delicately."

"And to put it indelicately?"

"Extremely pissed off, you could say. Which reminds me, would you like to wash up and have a bite of lunch?"

Morrison hesitated. "Well, fine, but on one condition. You come out with me for dinner someday soon."

"I thought you'd never ask." She stood. "Come on into the kitchen. We can keep talking while I see what I've got in the house." She sagged briefly. "To tell you the truth, I've been thinking about Jason so much, I've sort of lost track of the kitchen. But we'll find something. Not, I promise you, canned spaghetti."

While Harriet put together sandwiches, they went on. She spoke about each of the three people unhappy about their business dealings, or lack thereof, with Jason Belding. "Billy is really a sweet young man," she said. "A little greedy, maybe, but he couldn't conceivably want to hurt his father, except in the ways every kid hurts his parents. I think Georgia, that's his wife, was after Billy to put the screws on Jason to sell out—she likes pretty things, you could say—but—well, it's impossible."

Morrison reserved judgment. Wives who liked pretty things had been known to make men act impossibly before.

"Henry Oostdyk is something else again. Everybody in town knows he needs money. It's an open secret. Not like you or I would need money, but like Imelda Marcos needs money when she's down to her last thousand pairs of shoes. Nobody's exactly worried about the family bank, but they all figure he'll be selling out to one of the big city banks before long. The Oostdyks are old money, and I'd say they still have enough of it, but no new cash is coming in. Henry's not talented that way."

"If he's got the family money, what's his problem? You got a little more mayonnaise? I like my sandwiches sloppy."

Harriet looked critically at Morrison's waistline as she passed the jar. "You ever think of cutting down on the mayo?"

"Yeah. Every year at Lent. That's when I think about it." He fished a substantial gob out of the jar while Harriet wondered to herself why so many men are so stubborn, as if they were taking a stand against something their mommas were telling them to do.

"I don't think Henry's got the problem. It's Mrs. Henry. Judith Oostdyk. She was born a Janvier, and when the Huguenot Janviers teamed up with the Dutch Oostdyks, it was like the Missouri River joining up with the Mississippi, and Judith has no intention of letting the mighty waters degenerate into a trickle. She figures she's in charge of Appleboro, and her duties weigh heavy as a reigning monarch's crown. What Judy Oostdyk loves more than anything in the world is to hear someone protest that she gives too much of herself. And that takes money, keeping up her first-lady position."

"And does she? Give too much of herself, I mean."

Harriet laughed. "She would, but more and more people turn and run the other way when they see her coming to ladle some out. She's chairperson of every local charity drive, heads up the library board, is a director of the county hospital—and a lot of us have begun to wish she'd let the community struggle along with a little less guidance from above. But I'm getting away from my point. The thing is that she does it to old Henry, too. She needs money to be Queen Judith, and I know she keeps up palace standards at home. I'd bet that Henry gets hell if he doesn't close the toilet seat when he leaves the bathroom, and you know in advance there'll be a chenille toilet seat cozy on top of the lid, quivering with gentility, ready to deny the function of the contraption underneath it.''

Morrison figured Harriet would spend the day on Judith Oostdyk if he let her. "Okay, let's close the lid on Mrs. Oostdyk and go on. You said Carl Van Houten?''

"Oh, yes. I was saving him for last. If I had to pick a candidate for murderer—and for murder, if it came to that—it'd be Carl. I've known him since he was a boy in Appleboro, and even then he showed great talent for being obnoxious. He wants this land deal badly because he needs to show us all that even if he came from poor people around here, he's top dog now. And I suppose he is. He certainly is the richest man around, and the shabbiest, too.''

"How shabby?''

Harriet shrugged. "Oh, it's no one thing in particular, but there are stories about houses built too close together on thin soil, so that one man's septic tank drains into the next guy's well. And not delivering as promised, insulation a little less than specified, sod for the lawns three months late. You know. Nothing so bad that it'd be worth anybody's while to sink money into a lawsuit, but too often a shade away from cheating. Sometimes I think that when the state gives the exams for realtors' licenses, they flunk out anybody who doesn't qualify as a psychopathic liar.

"And the coarsest, crudest individual you can imagine. I remember that as a boy he would walk down Main and belch on demand, one of his greatest talents, and in fact the only one, far as I could ever see, and generally displayed for the edification of any old woman who happened to be walking by herself. I think he felt that bodily explosions were some kind of proof of manhood. These days he goes in for diamond pinky rings and Countess Mara neckties. He also cleans his nails compulsively and publicly with a fancy silver nail file, monogrammed, no less. Ugh!"

"Me, I get my ties at the Salvation Army."

"That's another problem. I thought you made them out of old quilts."

The afternoon wore on. When the mantel clock struck four, Morrison stood. "Damn! The day's getting away. I've got to get back to the desk."

"Tell me, what does a policeman have to do at a desk so much?"

"File reports," Morrison said glumly.

"File reports? About what?"

"File reports about what he'd be doing if he didn't have to file so many reports about it."

"I see," Harriet said in a voice indicating she didn't.

"Look, I know you've got more to tell me, so how's about we take it up again over that dinner? How about tonight? You free?" His face felt hot; he hoped he wasn't blushing.

"Free? I think I can arrange it," Harriet said wryly. "I'll call up my date and beg off. Thanks."

"See you about seven." He left.

At six-thirty Hugh Morrison found himself, un-characteristically, not able to decide what to do. He was taking an informant out to discuss a case and was entitled to use a police car, white with a flasher on top. But if this was a dinner engagement with a woman named Lorimer whom he had just met, his own beat-up Pontiac might be more appropriate. Friendlier. He chose the Pontiac. He also decided to go to a restaurant west of Appleboro, even though everybody around invariably headed either north toward Kingston, the county seat, or east across the Hudson to Poughkeepsie, the area's big town. Then there was the problem of the car radio. He normally kept it set to a station that played what they called golden oldies. Gershwin, Porter. Like that. Since Harriet had raised a kid, he wondered whether she was up on this stuff they broadcast out of Woodstock, music that went along with words he was never comfortable with, like *holistic* and *macrobiotic,* music for sitars and samisens. Maybe she liked the all-news station? He decided to leave the radio off. He also decided not to ask himself the significance of these momentous decisions.

At seven, Harriet heard a horn tooting. She looked out and saw a Pontiac and wondered why he had brought his own car and not the police car. She remembered back to her college days when a lady in a Henry James story— *Portrait of a Lady,* she thought it was—went into a room and saw her husband standing by the fireplace instead of sitting in his favorite chair, and this led to a two-hundred-page incomprehensible analysis of the nuances of his stance and to the ultimate dissolution of a marriage. She decided not to ask herself the significance of the Pontiac. Later, she also decided the reason for their heading in a direction no one in Appleboro ever took for dinner was none of her business.

In the restaurant, they talked a little more of the people Morrison should meet up with. "Elfrida Von Hesse may be useful," Harriet said. "She's got no stake in any of this, but she knows Appleboro better than anyone else around. She's the town historian and keeper of the flame. She runs the library, too, and that's where you'll find her most days. The only difficulty with Elfie is that she'll defend to the death the actions and virtues of anybody who had family in the area before 1700. The listener's death, I mean—from boredom.

"And Ben Stoddard. He's good for the unofficial history. He's the town gossip. What's out in the open, Elfie knows. What's undercover, and even under the covers, Ben knows. In fact, you have to be a little careful when you listen to him. There are those who think his portrait wouldn't be out of place as the frontispiece in a proctology

84

manual. He's got all the dirt, but the trouble is that what he doesn't have he makes up, for a more aesthetically satisfying story, malicewise, that is. For years he tried to find something, anything, that would have located Jason Belding in my bed, and barring that, something that would have taken me over to Jason's."

Morrison forebore asking the obvious question despite his interest in the answer. "Well, I think you've given me enough, more than enough, to start with. Why don't we settle back and enjoy the rest of the evening?"

"I'm enjoying it right now," Harriet said, "but I know what you mean. And I agree. Tell me, do you come here often for dinner? It's quite nice."

"No, not much. The police have an arrangement with the manager. We come here for our shady rendezvous and he gives us a group discount."

An hour and a half later, Morrison took Harriet home and saw her in the door. Awkwardly, he planted a modest kiss on her cheek. Inside, Harriet inadvertently caught a glimpse of herself in the pier glass and plummeted back to reality. With the shade of a twisted smile on her lips, she spoke to her reflection. "And while we're on the subject, old girl, what you need is a pier glass cozy."

As for Morrison, he had no time for such self-indulgent wistfulness. When he arrived home, he found a message on his answering machine. Pettit had found a spot in the field near the Belding place where the weeds hadn't grown up. He had also found a nail file and clippers in a fancy case on the same site, with the initials CVH stamped in gold on the leather. "I thought you'd want to know right away," the message ended.

CHAPTER 17

April 27: Poison Ivy

THE LIBRARY OPENED at two but as usual was quiet during the afternoon except for the gaggle of schoolchildren taken in at three and herded to the back room for story hour. A teacher read aloud, encouraged the kiddies to take turns reading to each other, and thereby ever so cleverly introduced them to the wonders of the Appleboro library and to the joys of reading. Sometimes this worked and sometimes it introduced the group more to the joys of pinching and snickering, but always it introduced shouting and squealing, and to openings of aspirin containers by Ms. Von Hesse.

Headache remedies could do nothing for her foul mood, however, and long after the children had departed and the better-behaved adults had started filing in after the workday was over, she continued to be on edge. To her dismay, Ben Stoddard was standing at her desk shortly after five. She smiled anyway, a martyr to propriety. "Hello, Ben. What can we do for you today?"

"The gemstone books, dear. Did you find any?"

Professional pride always took precedence over personal feeling with Elfie. "As a matter of fact, yes, I did.

I've got them tucked away for you and you can either take them out or look at them here.''

"Oh, thanks, love. You're a sweetheart. I'll look at them here.'' Ben took the five volumes that Elfie produced, two of which were quite large, and spread them out on a reading table. He opened the two large ones to the color plates and leafed through, finally grinning and nodding with obvious delight. Having found what he was looking for, he next turned to the indices of the other books and flipped pages rapidly, even greedily, devouring the contents with his eyes and wagging his head. "Elfie,'' he said, "look at this. It's called a black star. Someone around here has a couple of these. You know these things. Who is it?''

Like everyone else in Appleboro, Elfie never told Ben Stoddard a blessed thing unless she knew why he wanted to know. Especially when he had that look on his face, bloodhound crossed with jackal. "I have no idea. Why do you ask?''

"Oh, nothing really. I've seen one lately, that's all. Only it was on a key ring. And I think one of our founding families is up to something, sweetheart, and you know me when it comes to basic research.''

"Basic research, my foot. Basic dirt, you mean. Don't expect me to make mud pies with you, you hear?'' She sniffed.

"Oh, pooh, Elfie, you like to dish the dirt as much as anyone else, Miss Elfrida Von High and Mighty. Come off it.''

Elfie came off it, and with a bang. "I'm tired. I've had a rotten day. For heaven's sake, take your filth and your filthy mouth out of here and let me be. Now, get out, damn it! I've got work to do.''

"Well, if that's the way it is, to hell with you, too, Madam Librarian. And you'll probably meet lots of your Dutch and Huguenot buddies once you're down there. Much more than in the other place, sweetheart. Good night, Elfie, but I won't say goodbye because this isn't the last of it. Some of your fine folk are up to something dirty, I'm sure of it, and if I find out what it is, well, lovey, old Ben will wipe it up with that cashmere sweater you like to talk about, off my hands, off my feet, and off any other part of my body I find it on! You should try it yourself, sweetiepie," he said in his thinnest and nastiest voice. "Wiping yourself with cashmere can be real kicky. Even rewarding, let me tell you!"

He stomped out, slamming the library door. Elfie seemed even thinner and bonier and more drawn than her usual self as she sat in solitary splendor in her do-it-yourself throne room. Suddenly she sobbed, just once, but harshly, and it sounded like a rake being dragged across a concrete walk.

While Ben was at the library, Art Jessup took the extreme step of making a long-distance call. All the way to New York City. Just after five, when the rates went down, but while maybe the man was still in his office. He had tried the local number, but a recording had told him that Van Houten had left for the city. He got through. "Mr. Van Houten," he said, "I've got somebody else interested in my property, but I told them I promised you already. You come to any decision? Because I've got to get back to this other fellow, tell him where things stand."

Van Houten smiled to himself; old Jessup must be getting twitchy. Under other circumstances, it might have been fun to see just how much lower he would go on his price, but to hell with it. "Sorry, Art, but I'm going ahead with the Oostdyk land. Glad to hear you got yourself another buyer. Lotsa luck with it." His grin got wider; at his age you'd think the old fool would realize he didn't have the talent to try fiddling with Carl Van Houten. "Got to go now. Thanks for calling." He hung up, shaking his head from side to side in delighted disbelief.

Art went into the kitchen, where Til was making a lemon meringue pie on order from Ben Stoddard. "Well, old girl," he said, "I guess we're stuck. Van Houten isn't going to take the place. He was laughing at me when he said it, too, like he didn't think I was smart enough to know. Or maybe he didn't give a hoot if I knew or not. I don't know, Til, I just don't know."

Til wiped her hands on her apron. "Don't you worry about nothing, Art. The Lord will provide. And the Lord knows about the Van Houten boy, too."

"He just worships money, that one. Never mind about the Lord."

"Ah, but the Lord minds about him. 'Ye shall not make with me gods of silver, neither shall ye make unto you gods of gold. For I am the Lord your God.' Remember that, Art. 'He scorneth the scorners; but he giveth grace unto the lowly.'"

"Yes, Til."

And while Ben Stoddard was at the library and Art Jessup was calling Carl Van Houten, Henry Oostdyk was getting home from the bank. He sank into his chair in the living room and sighed deeply.

"Bad day, Henry?" Judith asked.

"No, just the usual. I'm very tired, that's all it is."

"Can I get you a drink? A little scotch?"

"I'd be out like a light. It'll be okay. I'll get myself an aspirin."

Henry lifted himself up and went into the bathroom to open the medicine cabinet. Neither of them used the downstairs cabinet much. There were some duplicates of what they kept upstairs, and old prescriptions tended to drift down and end up here rather than in the garbage pail. "Judith," he complained, "have you been straightening up in here, damn it?"

"Stop it now. I haven't opened up that cabinet in a week. Maybe more. What are you looking for?"

"Nothing. Damn it, you're always neatening things.

Move this, change that, don't put that down there. Why the heck don't you leave things alone!"

"I haven't done a thing. If you're thinking you can take it out on me when something goes sour the bank, you've got another think coming! If you want to tell me what's wrong, try doing it a little more civilly."

Henry's shoulders sagged. "I'm sorry."

"That's all right. I understand. Now I can tell you. I had the bridge crowd in about a week ago. That's the last visitors we've had. And you know what that means."

"Ben Stoddard? Him, rummaging around in the john?"

Judith nodded. "Ben Stoddard. Of course it was him. Who else?"

"Damn the man. I'm sorry I got so upset. I should have guessed it. That little weasel has moved everything in there all over the place. Look, Judy, I've got to simmer down by myself or I'm going to be miserable company this evening. I'll go out for a walk, maybe catch a show. You mind? I don't want to be yelling at you."

"Not at all. I haven't started dinner anyway. You come back anytime you get yourself relaxed. Give me a kiss and skedaddle."

Henry obeyed. Once he was out the door, Judith decided she'd clear out the medicine chest. They'd never use most of that old junk again, and it was no wonder the sight of it made Henry so nervous. Taking a grocery bag from the kitchen, she went into the bathroom and took the ancient garbage off the shelves. Most of it—pills, empty antiseptic bottles, dried-out Band-Aids—she dropped straight into the brown paper bag, but it was always useful to have a few empty vials around to tuck aspirin and things into when they traveled, so she opened several to dump out their contents. Catching a glimpse of a foreign object as she poured out the third container, she stopped to fish it out of the bag. Recognizing it, she frowned in puzzlement as she dropped it into the pocket of her cardigan. Later, back in

90

the living room, she sat down and turned it about in her hand as if looking for something, but whatever that something was—a secret message, a hidden compartment, a key to buried treasure—she couldn't fathom. What the dickens was Henry doing with this? she asked herself.

Henry consciously tried relaxing as he walked down Main, willing his shoulder muscles to loosen and turning his head from side to side to ease the throb in his neck. He saw Ben Stoddard explode out of the library—the man must have been in a dreadful rush—and he went inside on a sudden impulse. It seemed to be empty, though, of course, Elfie was there.

"Good evening, Elfrida," he said, and noting the twisted handkerchief the librarian was dabbing her eyes with, he added, "Or is it? Anything wrong, my dear?"

"No, nothing. I'm upset, that's all. I'm afraid I lost my temper and ordered Ben Stoddard out of here. You know what a dirty-minded little snoop he is, and I simply have had enough nonsense for today."

"Indeed I do know about Ben." Henry sat in the chair that Ben had vacated so hurriedly, and his eye took in the opened volumes on the table. He saw the color plates of gemstones. "Ben looking at these?"

"Yes. Something about black stars. They're really a cheap nothing of a stone, but that man is out to make trouble for somebody. He as much as said so. My God, but he can be such a vindictive little beast!"

"What's he up to?" Henry asked.

Elfie slapped the desktop with a determined hand. "I just don't want to talk about it, Henry. I've had enough for today. I'm very upset, and I wish you'd go, too."

"Why, Elfie, can't we even talk?"

"You know the answer to that perfectly well. No, we can't even talk. That's been the way you've wanted it for a quarter of a century—my God, has it been that long?—and that's the way it's going to be. Leave me alone.

We can talk when there are other people around and that's it. You can go now, Henry."

"Oh, Elfie, after all these years? Surely you're over all that. I don't understand."

"No, you certainly don't. Of course, I'm over all that. Don't flatter yourself, Henry Oostdyk. You're a damned fool if you've any idea that I'm some sort of Victorian ninny mooning all my life long over something like you. I don't feel anything for you, believe me, and if I did, it wouldn't be much more than a mild distaste, the way I'd feel about a flea-bitten stray that got in here and expected to be petted. You made your choice back then. Fine. Now stick with it."

"For heaven's sake, Elfie—"

"No, not for heaven's sake. For my sake and for Judith's sake, get out of here. I like Judy. She's my friend. You're my friend's husband, but I don't care for you very much." Henry looked as if he was about to object. She slapped the desk again. "I'm not going to discuss it anymore. Just get yourself out of here. And you're not welcome back, not alone, anyway."

Her eyes followed him as he went into the hall. He looked like that stray dog. She heard him open and close the door. And then she saw old Mrs. Parmenter, her arms loaded with the large-print books the poor thing came in for every week.

Elfie wondered how long she had been standing there and decided she'd better make sure Henry's visit appeared normal before the woman's tongue started wagging. "Dear Mrs. Parmenter. I didn't see you! Please do sit down and I'll check your books out soon's I make a call I keep forgetting about." She dialed. "Hello, Judith. Listen, Henry was just in and it simply slipped my mind completely to ask him to remind you that we've got to get your okay on that order slip for stationery. The one I gave you last Wednesday. We'll be writing on scraps of Kleenex if we don't get some paper soon. Thank you, dear. Tomorrow, then. And by the way, I think that you-know-who, our gossipy bridge partner, is on the hunt for dirt again. You know who." She looked at Mrs. Parmenter, who in her turn was trying to look bored while she drank in every word. "Something to do with a black star. Black star, like Betty Belding's earrings, remember? Anyway, it's *en garde,* and *sauve qui peut,*" she finished with a false and tinkly little laugh.

"Do excuse me, Mrs. Parmenter. Now let's see about these books of yours." Well, she thought bitterly, maybe covering my tracks will keep me young. Lord knows, this has got me acting like the damned fool I was twenty-five years ago. She put her head to one side. Or was it nearer to thirty? Where have the years gone, except right down the drain?

Henry continued walking down Main, his neck and shoulders throbbing with pain again. He was too tired to walk, too tired to go home, where he knew he'd be snapping at Judith even if the poor girl hadn't done anything. He passed the movie house, the Joy Rio. The show was about to start and he turned abruptly, bought a ticket, and went in. He was the only patron over nineteen in the place, it seemed to him as he surveyed the hallful of kids slumped down on their spines, their feet clad in filthy canvas shoes that they dangled arrogantly over the seats in front. He stared at the screen as the house went dark, sweating in the cool room, a stranger in his own town, trapped amid the alien (and rancid) popcorn in the foul air.

It was a night for the telephone, particularly at the Lorimer place. First it was Ben Stoddard calling. After a moment of giggling amenities, he got to the point. "Listen, dear, I've got to send my niece a graduation present and I thought of a hunk of jewelry of some kind, a bracelet or earrings, maybe. And it seems to me someone around here has something set with a black star and I think that's a stone that looks expensive, costs cheap, and sounds like a good idea. Do you remember who or what? I'm not sure but I think I might have seen it at the Oostdyks. Anyway, I'd like to find out."

"Oh, sure," Harriet said. "But I don't think it was at the Oostdyks. Jason had a couple of black stars, but that won't help you, because he picked them up in India years ago. He had them made into earrings for Betty, and after she went, he had one put into a key ring so's he'd always have it with him."

"Poor dear Jason."

"Yes." Sympathetic sounds from Ben irritated her. "Elfie and I helped him pick a setting. But that doesn't help you much. I'm sure any jewelry store can tell you whatever you want to know. As you say, they're not very expensive and they look quite elegant."

"Elfie knows about them, hey? Maybe I'll ask her. Thanks so much, dear." His voice sounded thin, the way it did when he thought he was saying something epigrammatic, when all he was doing was only being his usual spiteful self. "See you soon."

No sooner had Harriet hung up than the phone rang again. It was Billy Belding calling from New York. "Hello, Aunt Harriet, how are you?"

"Pretty fair, Billy. And you?"

"Well as can be expected. But listen, maybe you can help. I don't know who Dad's lawyer was, and I don't think his will is in the house up there. Maybe you can tell me whom to contact. I'd like to get hold of it soon as possible."

Harriet hesitated. "His lawyer. I'm quite sure he used Judson Connor up in Kingston. We all of us do for things like that. Anyway, give it a try." She didn't add that she knew Judson Connor was in Europe and the probability was that the cretinous child who worked for him wouldn't have been able to find the tip of her nose without a guidebook.

There was something else she didn't add and as

94

soon as Billy was off the phone, she called Hugh Morrison.
All this phoning, she thought, and how lucky it was that as
a widow and an orphan she had telephone shares in what
the broker grandly called her portfolio. "Hugh! I didn't interrupt you at anything like a can of spaghetti, did I?"

"That's all right, reheated spaghetti is one of my
favorite things. What's up?"

"Billy Belding just called. He's looking for his father's will, and there's something I didn't tell him. And that
I didn't tell you." Morrison, out of long police habit of letting others feel forced to fill in the gaps, most often in
order to encourage them to tie themselves in knots, kept
silent. "The thing is, I've got the will, right here in the
house."

"Why didn't you tell the poor devil, Harriet? He's
probably going crazy wondering where it is."

"Because I was scared."

"Scared of what?"

"Oh, Hugh, because I know what's in it. Jason left
it all in trust for the grandchildren, and I'm the executor
and I'm the trustee or whatever you call it. He said I had
more sense than Billy and that I'd do right by the land. If I
say so, they can put a road across Jason's land for that Van
Houten development, and if I say they can't, they can't.
And I'm not going to let them do it. The kids get the property when they're of age, and until then, they'll develop
that land over my—"

"You were perfectly right. You could be in deep
trouble, Harriet. Say nothing for as long as possible, which,
damn it, probably won't be for too long. Hold tight, old
girl."

Harriet's hand was gripping the arm of the chair she
was sitting in. Her knuckles were white. "Don't worry. I
will," she said. "I am." And to herself, she added that she
was getting awfully tired of being scared.

CHAPTER 18

April 28: Wild Geranium

*M*ORRISON WAS ON his Senior Investigator dignity for the trip down to New York, wearing the suit that exited the closet only a few times a year, the one that didn't come from the discount store, and the Liberty silk necktie left over from the days when Marie used to make him dress up on holidays. He had arranged to speak to Carl Van Houten, who was in his city office for the week, and to Billy Belding at his place in some building with a name as well as a street number. He sensed, from what Harriet had told him, that the job might be easier if he didn't turn up in Van Houten's backyard looking like one of the bumpkins the man figured he had left behind.

He took the bus down, which was simpler than going in by car, and he walked down West Forty-second Street, a pilgrimage he always enjoyed: It made him feel more content about the life of an upstate cop. Besides, looking at the titles of the newest porno flicks was always educational. Today they were featuring, among others, something called *Beneath the Bishop's Canonicals.* It was a warm day and the bracing scent of urine was in the air. Morrison walked quickly.

He took the subway down to Twenty-third and walked over to Van Houten's office on Fifth, below the highest-rent district but giving a real estate outfit an address that sounded classy, at least to out-of-towners.

An elevator with a chipped gray-enamel interior rattled dispiritedly as it groaned through a passage to the third floor and deposited him in Van Houten's reception room, where a woman at a typewriter pulled back a finger-smudged glass panel and asked him his business. She directed him to take a seat, which he did, and he riffled through a prospectus for a condo he couldn't afford in a far-off state he didn't want to live in. The pictures of the condo, costly town houses, featured handsome slender mommies and handsome slender daddies and happy golden kiddies. Every damned one of them displayed a broad, toothy, idiot grin as they stood proudly in front of their condo contemplating their handsome slender Mercedes. "Fuck you, too," he suggested silently.

The rest of the waiting room was of even less interest. He picked up one item, a small and dusty vase that supported a dispirited paper rose, and turned it around in his hand. The receptionist said, "Nice, isn't it? That's called Leerdam crystal. Mr. Van Houten's people came from Leerdam, originally. That's in Holland. He thought it would be a lovely touch for the office."

"Lovely," Morrison agreed faintly as he sat back and sighed impatiently, wishing he could render himself semiconscious while he waited.

Once the detective was inside Van Houten's office, the man himself came from behind the desk and extended a hand. "Good to see you, sir. Since your call, I've been racking my brains and I still don't see how I can help, but I'm happy to tell you anything I can. Please, have a seat." He smiled with the same sappy sincerity of the gentry in the condo brochure.

Morrison sank into a comfortable chair, something that would relax a potential client, and looked around. The

97

walls were not shabby like the rest of the premises and were liberally endowed with photographs of homes, shopping centers, certificates that looked like awards, and presentation scenes in which Van Houten was front and center accepting plaques and scrolls.

Van Houten watched the detective. "Story of my life," he said modestly.

"Yes. Well, as I said, we're talking to everyone who knew Mr. Belding well or who was involved in this real estate hassle with him at the time of his death."

"Sure, I understand. And you're absolutely right."

So glad to have your approval, sir, Morrison thought. He said, "Yes." Then he cleared his throat. "Mr. Van Houten, I'd like to know just what this deal for the Oostdyk land meant to your organization."

"A lot of money, Mr. Morrison, much Mazola, I kid you not. I'll be perfectly frank. I wanted that land and I invested maybe ten, twenty thou in it before I knew we had hit a snag. Something like that anyway. That's a straight answer."

Morrison decided that the man knew precisely to the penny how much he had sunk into the operation, but he let it go, except as it confirmed his impression that beneath this frank and helpful exterior lurked a little fellow who wasn't going to tell him a damn thing unless it was squeezed out of him. "Doesn't sound like too much for a major operation like yours," he said. "Or is it?"

"I have to contradict you there. In a cutthroat game like this, sometimes it looks like a ten-cent differential can give a guy a competitive edge. But it wouldn't have hurt me much, if that's what you mean. Hell, I'd even have got some of it back, a lot of it, by carting out the lumber stored up the hill behind Belding. I don't know why the man was so stubborn." He shook his head. "You'd think I was putting up a glue factory, for God's sake! Anyway, I'd have lost some on labor, a lot of the lumber that's cut to spec, stuff the workmen steal—the sons of bitches always rob a guy blind and you've got to figure it in the cost. That's about it. I'd have trucked things down to the Jessup place and started construction there. Simple as that. No pain. No sweat." He sat back contentedly, took out a combination nail file and clippers and began digging under his well-manicured nails.

"I see. So Mr. Belding's attitude was a disappointment, something of a loss, but not a disaster. That right?"

"You got it." He looked at his watch.

"Just a couple of other things, then. First, I need to know where you were last December fifth. I realize that's asking a lot, but try to reconstruct it if you can."

"Doris!" the man bawled. "Look in the cabinet and see if you can find last year's calendar!" He smiled at the detective. "Keep these things for years, until the cabinets get stuffed. You never know. The IRS, that kind of bull, right?" Doris came in with the pages of a desk calendar neatly held together with rubber bands. "Let's see. I tell you true that this is a slim chance, but let's have a look." He turned pages toward the end of the stack. He laughed. "Hey, this is a hoot! That whole week I was in San Juan at a builders' convention. At La Concha in the Condado section. You know it?" Morrison shook his head. "Beautiful island. Overbuilt, though. These damn speculators. Anyway, Doris'll have all the bills and receipts from the airlines and the hotels to back me up. Have to keep them for Uncle Sam. Wish I didn't, but don't we all. You want I should have her make you copies?" He consulted his watch for a second time.

"In time, but for now your word'll do. Now, for the other thing: May I see your nail file there? Just for a moment. Very handsome," he said to Van Houten's puzzled face, "but this one's got more class, wouldn't you say?" He took the file and leather case that Bob Pettit had found out of his pocket and tossed it on the desk.

Van Houten reached toward it. "Don't touch, please," Morrison said. "Evidence. You understand."

"Hey, man, I don't get it. I thought the thing was lost. How'd you get hold of it?"

"Found it, Mr. Van Houten. Found it in a field."

"Great! So what's the big deal? What's this evidence business about?"

"You see, we found it on the Belding property, and in view of the circumstances, there's the question of how you happened to lose it there."

"Hell, I go through that place regularly. That's what it's all about, buddy. I've got to go through it to get to the parcel I figured to put this damned development on. You know the story good as me. Come on, now," he said with a show of irritation.

"No, sir, you come on. You've been looking at your watch, sir, and I guess you don't have any time to waste. Neither do I. My boss doesn't like me to kick around too much down here in New York. Thinks maybe I'll enjoy myself. Taxpayers don't like it, either." Morrison leaned forward toward Van Houten. "Let's cut the cackle. We found that file right where there was no grass growing, no weeds. Then we found Jason Belding's body, what was left of it, anyway, maybe fifty, seventy-five yards away, and funny thing, but there was lots of grass and weeds right under it, like it hadn't been there too long." He sat back again. "So some of our boys, they got suspicious minds, comes from hanging around the criminal element too much, I suppose, and they got to wondering if maybe somebody moved the body from one place to another. And there was this fancy file of yours. We figured we owed it to ourselves to ask you about it, Mr. Van Houten."

Van Houten's face was an angry red. "You accusing me of murder? Is that it? That's nuts, man!"

"Oh, perish the thought, sir. You seem to have proof that you were nowhere near the scene of the original crime." He stressed the word "original." "But, of course, the corpse was moved, and you're connected with that in some way. No, we're not accusing you of murder." He

100

smiled, without parting his lips. "Not at this time, any-way."

"I don't know I ought to be speaking to you without a lawyer."

"That's your prerogative, sir." Morrison sat and waited, watching Van Houten's expression range from doubt to belligerence and back via a puzzled frown.

"Tell you what, Officer. I've got something pretty much gets me out of this. I let you have it, you think we can clear things up?"

"I can't promise anything, but if you think it'll help me, you can be sure it'll help you, sir. But no promises."

"Doris! Get me all the tapes we've made in the last couple of weeks." He turned to Morrison. "Hate to do this to a buddy, but what the hell, murder's not my bag, you know what I mean. Good citizen, crap like that, right down the line." He drummed his fingers on the desk. "Doris! Move it, babe, will you!"

Doris hove into sight, half a dozen cartridges in her hand. "I can't fly, Mr. Van Houten. I had to look for them, didn't I?"

"Okay, okay, sorry if I upset you. Powder your nose or go to lunch or something, will you? The officer and I would like a little privacy."

"It's just after eleven, Mr. Van Houten. If I take off now, I won't be back till one-thirty, two. I want you should understand that."

Van Houten waved her out brusquely. "Okay, but just go." Morrison figured that one day, right after she was paid, Doris wasn't going to come back at one-thirty, two, or any other time, and silently he wished her well.

"Now," Van Houten said, "look at this here. Any-time I get a call I think I ought to have a record of, I flip this little switch, then that little switch, and I get it all down on one of these cassettes. This gizmo goes with me every-where." He looked through the cassettes while he talked. "This is the one I want you to hear. I hate to do this, but if there's anything criminal going on, Carl Van Houten don't want any part of it, right? The next voice you hear will be that of Mr. William Belding, son of the late Jason Belding. That's pretty good, hey? I sound like a TV anchor man." He grinned. "New career, huh?"

Morrison listened to the tape and heard Billy Belding ask Van Houten to bring a tarpaulin over to his place, and then say he'd explain when Van Houten got there. "Interesting," he said when it was over. "I'd like a copy of that."

"A pleasure. And you know what I saw when I got there. Gets me off the hook, all right."

"In part," Morrison agreed blandly, "but concealing a crime, well, you've still got a problem, sir."

"Concealing a crime! Hell, that was exposing a crime, man. The reason Belding did it is that he figured the old man had been there for months and nobody'd found him, and what he wanted was for it to be found, so's we could get on with our business."

"One small correction: What you both wanted was for Jason Belding to be found. But we can overlook that for now."

"So what do you think? I'm off the hook, huh?"

Morrison crossed his legs casually. "Well, not entirely, as I explained. But I'll tell you what. You give me that tape and you give up any idea of calling William Belding soon as I leave here, and I can say we'll take it easy with you. But if I get the slightest hint, just the slightest, that you contacted the man before I get to him, and— Listen, I could look up what the law says about helping a criminal conceal a murder and let you have a copy. How's that strike you?"

Van Houten held up a hand. "No, I get it. You got me by the short hairs and I know it. And believe me, there's not many can say they got Carl Van Houten that way. Trust me. My phone is disconnected until you say so." He raised his right hand and took the boy scout pledge.

"Good. Now if you let me have that tape, I'll be off."

"Right you are. Pleasure to do business with you."

Morrison did not say "Likewise, I'm sure." He said, "Yeah," and he left. He did not extend a hand to Van Houten, nor did Van Houten extend one to him. He did, however, nod brusquely.

The appointment with Belding wasn't until two, which left plenty of time to kill. Morrison liked Manhattan; it was ratty and run-down; it was filled with madmen, some of whom shouted obscenities at every passerby; and the garbage was knee-deep. But the city pulsed and vibrated with life. The realization that any other town would be unable to absorb the sights and sounds of New Yorkers, that Washington, D.C., for instance, would probably clap half the population of Manhattan in the pokey on sight was a big plus for the old town. What a place. He subwayed uptown to the apartment that he and Marie had been in on West Seventy-first and stared at the building. Inside the lobby, he inspected the buzzers. There were four Spanish names squeezed onto the nameplate for his old pad. Outside again, he went up to the shops on Seventy-second. His favorite bakeries were gone; only the old Viennese one, where the pastries were poised to dispense instant cardiac arrest to anyone over forty, was there, its lethal wares displayed in the window. The ratty old neighborhood stores were gone as well, replaced by hideously trendy monstrosities called boutiques.

He bought a hot dog and an orange drink and plodded sadly back down Broadway; he never should have looked again, except with his mind's eye. "Stupid old flatfoot," he muttered, and then looked around guiltily, wondering whether anyone might think he was one of the natives babbling merrily as he slouched along the street. Realizing that no one in this town would admit to noticing anything, he straightened up, strode forth vigorously, and tried to look like a busy executive, alert, purposeful, and fully aware of what the hell he was up to, and, like everybody else, just a little bit afraid.

CHAPTER 19

April 28: Mustard

UNLIKE VAN HOUTEN, Belding worked in a building that was new, shiny, possibly efficiently designed, and devoid of even what little individuality might derive from peeling elevator interiors. Morrison decided he preferred Van Houten's surroundings, though not by much. A less harried secretary escorted him back to Belding's office. (Medium large, room for couch, view of Chrysler Building, but containing metal file cabinet, no corner window, and no conference table: executive, but not quite senior.)

Belding, mid-thirties to forty, trim in a gray pinstripe, took off a pair of rimless glasses and stood, extending a hand toward Hugh Morrison. "I'm glad you're here, Mr. Morrison. I want so much to know if you've made any progress."

"A little. But it isn't going to be easy, and we need all the help you can give us. It's going to be necessary to question everybody—friends, family, everybody—as if they were likely suspects. It's the only way we can go."

Billy nodded. "I understand. Let's sit over here." He waved Morrison onto the couch and took an armchair next to it. "Okay? Let's go."

104

"Well, let's start backward." He smiled. "Do you have any questions for me?"

"No, nothing beyond who did this to Dad. Well, maybe one other thing. Dad's will. Did you come across it? I assume you went through the house. It's sort of an embarrassment because we can't get anything settled until we find it."

"Didn't he have a lawyer?"

"Yes, but the man's on vacation and his office doesn't know a blessed thing. Anyway, people don't necessarily leave their wills with a lawyer. Personally, I've got mine at home."

"Can't help. Sorry. If anything turns up, we'll be in touch right off. Anything else?"

"Not at the moment. I can't think of a thing."

"Okay, then I'll begin. First, I know it was a long time ago, but do you have any records that would show where you were on last December fifth."

"December fifth? Is that when my father was killed?"

Morrison reproved him gently. "My turn to ask the questions, Mr. Belding."

"I don't know offhand, but we save the old calendars for several years in case the IRS wants to challenge us on deductions. Hold it a sec." He opened the office door and looked out. "Liz," he said, "be a sweetheart and see if you can get last December's calendar out of the storeroom. I'll dust you off when you get back."

Morrison heard the woman laugh. "No way, buddy. Any dusting to do, my husband will do it."

"Foiled again," Belding said as he came back in and closed the door. "My secretary'll be right in. Like a cup of coffee?"

"Thanks. Black, two sugars."

When his secretary came in, Belding took the calendar and gave the coffee order. "Okay, I guess we're set. Lizzie'll have the coffee in a minute. Meantime, I'll take a look at this thing." He turned through the stack of sheets. "Yeah, here it is. Hey, we're in luck; December fifth last year I was in Boston. Copley Plaza, December four, until the sixth. Client meeting. Take a look?"

"No, not necessary. Can you make a copy of that page for me? If you've got the airline stubs, I'd like a copy of them, as well. And I'll need to know how to get in touch with the clients you were with."

"You bet." The secretary brought in coffee and set it on Belding's desk. As she bent over with the cups, Morrison noted, mechanically, that she was a couple of sizes smaller in the waist than Van Houten. He sighed, stirred his coffee, and slurped the hot liquid noisily. Belding, after directing his Lizzie to get the copies Morrison wanted, sipped quietly. "What else can I tell you?"

"Have you ever heard of the Enoch Arden law, Mr. Belding?"

"I've heard the name, but I don't honestly recall knowing what it is. Why do you ask?"

Morrison ignored the question. "Tell me, when did you first find out that your father was dead?"

"I don't understand. When you called me and told me what had happened, of course."

"Funny. You ask different people the same question and you get different answers. This is a tough business. First, I hear you were in the Appleboro library asking for books about the Enoch Arden law. The way I understand it, this law is something about how long you have to wait before you can declare a person legally dead, put the will through probate, that sort of thing."

"Oh, yeah, that's right! Well, you see, uh, it's sort of embarrassing and my wife and I, I mean I thought, uh, uh, maybe if Dad—"

Morrison waved a hand in dismissal. "Doesn't matter, doesn't matter." What mattered was that he had thrown the man off balance, no matter how slightly. It was time to move ahead. He put his coffee cup back on the

106

desk, placed his two hands on his thighs—neatly covering the spot of coffee that had landed on his right leg—and leaned toward Belding. "What I'm more interested in is whether there's something else you maybe forgot. The way I hear it, you found your father's body a couple of days before I told you about it."

"That's crazy. Of course not."

"Well, you see, the way Mr. Van Houten tells it, you told him you were ready to go ahead and sell him this right-of-way or whatever you call it across the land. And that was before you knew, say you knew, you had inherited."

"The man's confused, doesn't know what he's talking about."

Morrison fished in his pocket. "I've got this thing here, this cassette, from Mr. Van Houten. I'd play it for you, but I'm a greenhorn around these gadgets and I'm afraid I'd wipe it out. But I've heard it for myself. It's your voice all right, asking the man if he could meet you at your father's place, bring along a tarpaulin, and you'd explain to him when he got there. Maybe you'd like to explain to me, too, like right now."

"This is ridiculous!"

"I agree. It's ridiculous. And you don't have to say a word. You don't even have to believe me when I tell you what's on this thing." He held up the cassette, wiggling it in the air, live bait for a poor fish. "If you like, you can call a lawyer. Up to you." He paused. "So what's it gonna be? Make up your mind, Mr. Belding. We're both busy men."

"Oh, God," Belding finally said, wiping his hand across his forehead. "I've been stupid. Yes, I found my father's—what was left of him. I only knew because of that old flight bag he carried around in the fields all the time, and those shoes. We gave him those shoes the Christmas before. Waterproof. L. L. Bean. My wife ordered them from the catalogue."

"We can skip the shoes, sir."

"What? Oh. Well, I realized that he'd been there for months, and nobody had found him. It could have been an eternity until— Look, I know it sounds cold-blooded, my own father, but what could I do? There wasn't any point in letting the property just sit there for years, like the Enoch Arden law says you have to. What could I do?"

"For one thing, you could have called the police."

"I know. I should have. But I was afraid they'd say that I did it, that I— What the hell, I panicked, that's all. I felt guilty, as if I had really done it. Or at least somehow willed it done. Is that a crime? I mean, they wouldn't have believed me if I said I took a walk to look at the place where I buried the cat, and just happened to find my father's body. I couldn't think straight. They wouldn't have believed me!"

"Maybe not. But you could think straight enough to move your own father's remains because there was money in it. That right? Maybe you should've buried him like the cat," Morrison said in a disgusted voice. "And anyway, what's this about a dead cat?"

Belding sucked his breath in deeply, involuntarily. He explained about finding the cat starved to death in the house. Then he said, "You've made your point, Mr. Morrison. But I could never have killed my own father. Ask anybody. Ask Mrs. Lorimer, for one."

"Mrs. Lorimer has told me about you. She thinks the world of you." Morrison paused. "She also thought the world of your father," he said quietly.

"Are you— Do you plan on telling her about this? Does she have to know about it?"

"What I plan on saying to Mrs. Lorimer or anybody else is something I can't dicuss. But let me say this: You panicked, or so you say. Well, that's no crime by itself. It's pretty damn stupid, but it's no crime," Morrison said soothingly. "On the other hand, concealing a crime is a crime. Moving a body is a crime. And speaking of that, what did you expect to accomplish, anyway?"

Belding's face reddened. "I figured if I moved him near the road, someone would find it, him, pretty soon. And time was important on account of this property deal. I'm sorry. I wish I could— What are you— What happens next?" He looked up anxiously.

"Nothing much. I check your story, for starters. Don't worry. You're not charged with murder. Not yet, anyway. Nothing happens." Morrison smiled sadly and stood. "I'll run along now. And by the way, if you have to go out of town, business trips or something, let us know first, will you? Thanks." He left.

Belding got behind his desk and dialed. "Doris, is your boss in?" He waited, biting at the eraser end of a pencil. He slapped the pencil down and spoke very softly into the phone. "You bastard," he said, "you stinking son of a bitch."

When Morrison got out into the sunny spring afternoon, he suddenly knew that he was too tired to think about the bus trip home right away. He needed time to breathe, some place dark and quiet. Some place to lie down would have been ideal. He treated himself, extravagantly for a cop, to a taxi back to Forty-second Street, and, feeling self-conscious while standing out in broad daylight at the ticket window, bought himself a ticket to *Beneath the Bishop's Canonicals*. He watched glumly for fifteen minutes, but the film was more boring than obscene, so he heaved himself out of the seat and shuffled wearily down the two blocks to the bus terminal and transportation home. He made notes to himself on the bus. Check the Boston hotel, the clients, and the airline, not that that would prove a damn thing; you could get from Boston to Appleboro in a few hours in a rented car, and then back again before anybody missed you, if you worked it right.

Half an hour later, he took out his pen and paper again: There were flights to and from San Juan so often that if the Lexington Avenue subway could sprout wings and fly off from South Ferry on the tip of Manhattan, they

109

could bring in enough to pay off the city's debts and still have lots left over to staff the mayor's payroll with a fresh complement of crooks. He told himself to check all flights on December 4, 5, and 6 between New York and San Juan, both ways. All of them, Eastern, United, Continental, any others, and look for a passenger name of Van Houten. It'd be almost as easy to get from San Juan to Appleboro and back before you were missed as from Boston to Appleboro. It was a wonderful world we were living in, Morrison observed.

CHAPTER 20

April 29: Gay Wings

GEORGIA BELDING FROWNED at her husband. "You know," she said, "if you hadn't been in such an all-fired hurry to get Dad's money, none of this would have happened." Billy had finished telling her about the visit from the police. "I don't see how you could have done it, really I don't."

"I suppose you can't, sweetheart. Of course, if I wasn't paying for damn near six pairs of shoes a day from Bloomie's, it sometimes looks like, maybe I wouldn't have been in this all-fired hurry of yours."

"How am I supposed to take that? It's my fault? Whatever you did, Billy, it's you that did it. Not me. Try to remember." She exaggerated the busywork of straightening the magazines on the coffee table.

"That's my little helpmeet for you, standing by my side when at the first hint of trouble . . ."

Georgia looked up. "Are you in trouble, Billy?" she asked. What she didn't ask was what kind of trouble, and how much.

It was only a little bank, and Henry Oostdyk's office was suitably modest. True, the desk was of a conscientiously polished wood, but only because Oostdyk's secretary appreciated her responsibilities. There were two straight-back chairs for visitors, but no couch and no upholstered pieces, not because this was an unfriendly bank but because there wasn't room for extras. The current building had been completed before the First World War, and the stern Dutch heritage of the proprietors did not include coddling, even of an Oostdyk. Which, of course, was one of the current Oostdyk's personal problems—Oostdyks were told from birth that they had to stand on their own two feet, but then nobody would let them do it.

At the moment one of the straight-back chairs was filled to overflowing by Senior Investigator Hugh Morrison.

"December fifth of last year? That's kind of difficult, unless there's something on the calendar." As had Belding and Van Houten, Henry Oostdyk enlisted the aid of his secretary. She brought in the prior year's desk calendar and opened it to the date in question.

"Anything else, Mr. Oostdyk?" she asked.

Her employer looked at her in surprise. "No, Helen, that'll be all, thank you." He failed to pick up the hint to offer the visitor a cup of coffee; banks don't give coffee, being more attuned to dealing with suppliants than with interrogators, and anyway, Grandpa Oostdyk had never said anything about serving coffee. "There's nothing here that'll tell us anything, I'm afraid. I had a lunch meeting with my top staff, but that's it."

Cops don't offend bank presidents, even meek ones, especially when it's the only bank president in town. "I have a couple more questions, but I want you to understand that they're things I have to ask of everyone connected to this land deal."

"Naturally. I'd be offended if you didn't." Oostdyk smiled; a stranger could reasonably have considered the smile apologetic.

"First, in the normal course of events, could you have left the office during the day for any period of time

112

without having noted it on the calendar? A business call, maybe to run an errand, anything like that?"

"No, I don't think so. I'm here, right in the office, nine to five every day without fail, unless it's on the calendar."

"I don't suppose there's any way we could check that."

Oostdyk spread his hands in a gesture of helplessness. The buzzer on his desk sounded. He picked up the phone. "Yes, Helen. Oh. By all means, do." He hung up and turned back to Morrison. "My secretary is looking for the time cards," he said, and catching the expression of surprise on the detective's face, he added, "All of us have punched in and out since my great-grandfather put the system in during the last century. From the highest to the lowest. All of us. What's right for one is right for all." He spoke firmly, sounding as if he was quoting great-grandfather directly, which he was.

Helen took the card in. Oostdyk looked at it and passed it over. "There you are, sir. In at ten to nine, out at almost five-thirty."

Morrison looked at the card. "I see." He handed it back. "The other thing is, would you have some way of knowing what you did that evening?"

Oostdyk laughed. "I could ask my wife, but, well, really!"

"Yeah. Sure." Morrison took his leave. On the way out, he stopped at the secretary's desk. "Listen, Miss, there's something I want to ask you. Do you punch Mr. Oostdyk in and out, like this is something you do for the boss, part of your job?"

"Oh, no, sir!" She looked shocked. "Mr. Oostdyk and his father before him were very firm about that. 'We're all employees of the bank,' Mr. Oostdyk senior used to say. Nobody waits on anybody else, and that includes punching the clock."

"Thanks." He left.

Pinky looked up as Morrison went into the station

house. "I got that poop you was interested in. Belding was registered the Copley Plaza in Boston both sides of December fifth. And the client meeting story checks out, morning and afternoon until three-thirty, four. 'Course he could've drove down here and back the same day easy." He reconsidered. "With a little trouble, maybe, but he could have. And your boy Van Houten's not on any airplane manifest between San Juan and New York anytime from the fourth to the sixth last December. Plus he's registered the whole week at this here hotel. La Coochie? That right?"

"Yeah. Thanks, Pinky." That left Oostdyk with lots of opportunity, Belding with opportunity with difficulty, and put Van Houten in the clear. So far as he could tell right now. If it was one of those three. If it happened on December 5. If.

Maybe, Morrison told himself later, he shouldn't have gone on to see the Von Hesse woman and the Stoddard man that same day, when he was tired. But he wanted to get on with things, for his own sake, for the sake of his job, and for Harriet, who he sensed wasn't going to relax until this was settled. As it was, he got nothing from either one. The Von Hesse, whom he bearded in her library den, was a bundle of prejudices: "Henry Oostdyk is as fine a man as you'd ever want to know, and I resent your insinuations." There was no point in explaining to her. "Billy Belding is a dear young man." And "Carl Van Houten is capable of anything, but I'm not going to gossip." She drew up shoulders up and shook them, as if to disengage the stain of the questions from her person. He pegged her as a citizen likely to demand police action at any opportunity, such as sighting dangerous felons throwing chewing-gum wrappers onto the sidewalk, yet equally likely to regard police interest in someone she knew socially as an intrusion equivalent to mounted Cossacks advancing with unsheathed sabers.

"Thank you, ma'am," Morrison said. "If you think of anything else, please let me know." He half-hoped she wouldn't. "I have an appointment with Mr. Benjamin Stoddard. Can you direct me to his house?"

She could and did. But Morrison sensed an amalgam of disapproval and tension in her expression. He felt she wanted to tell him something but couldn't bring herself to anything so vulgar as confiding in a peasant.

Mr. Benjamin Stoddard was just as uninformative, but in a different way. "Oh, my dear boy, Carl Van Houten would do anything for money. . . . Billy Belding's wife gets rid of money like yesterday's newspaper. . . . Henry Oostdyk would jump off the roof if his wife ordered him to, and I wouldn't be surprised if she did." He sat back happily. "Of course, I'm fond of the Belding boy, and both the Oostdyks are dear friends, but it's my duty, isn't it?"

He continued to do his duty, to the disadvantage of his dear friends, for several happy minutes, until Morrison interrupted. "Is there anything more specific, Mr. Stoddard?" Stoddard had so far called him his dear boy three times; once more and it was going to be a choice between an antacid pill for himself or a fat lip for this gabbling fool.

"Well, dear boy, I shouldn't talk out of school . . ."

"Yes, you should, Mr. Stoddard," Morrison said irritably. "This is a police matter."

"Oh, you're so right. What I mean is that there's been talk about the Oostdyks being a leetle bit hard up for cash these days, and this land deal means a lot to them. Little things, like serving dollar-twenty-nine-a-pound mushrooms for lunch, not traveling the way they used to." He sat back, but then, happy to have thought of something more, leaned forward and added, almost confidentially, "Saving tiny slivers of soap. You know?"

Morrison knew, so he left, telling himself that one day when he was fresher, he'd go back and put this creep through the wringer. The man might even know something but want to hold on to it like a kid with his last piece of candy. This kind always had a last piece of candy to clasp in his hot, moist hand, sniff, fondle, and then even return to his pocket for future fun and games.

Ben picked up the phone and dialed the library. "Hello, sweetie, guess who was just here! Oh, you know." His voice was thick with disappointment. "Not much. I mean, why should I gossip about our friends? Like Henry Oostdyk and that black star. And by the way, you've been very naughty, Elfrida Von Hesse. You knew all along about that black star, didn't you? Shame on you, sweetheart, you helping Jason get a setting for it, and then trying to fool an old friend like poor little I! I'm not like that myself, and I won't hold out on you, dear. I happen to know who's got that black star, and if his initials are H.O., I wouldn't be at all surprised. You know, maybe it was wrong of me not to tell that poor sap of a policeman. You think I should call him up and confess? We've got to be good citizens, honey, don't we? Hm?"

Enough is enough, even for a proper lady. "You're not a good citizen, Ben Stoddard. You're, you're a mess the dog has made in the house; you're filth!"

As Ben snapped back something about wiping up the mess with that cashmere sweater, Elfrida slammed the phone down, furious that this man had goaded her so successfully. She knew the little weasel was hugging himself with delight this very moment. After a slight hesitation, she dialed the Oostdyk house; it was nearly six and they'd both be home.

Ben Stoddard was dialing, as well. He reached Harriet Lorimer and told her how worried he was about dear Elfrida. "You know, dear, she's had a crush on Henry Oostdyk for half a lifetime, and we both know about Henry's financial troubles, don't we, and I think it's driving Elfie bonkers. . . . Now, don't you talk that way, Harriet. I could even tell you the motel those two stayed at—of course, it was long before Judith was on the scene—and if the old room clerk is still there, which is pretty doubtful, I suppose—"

Harriet never was a proper lady. "You're a horse's ass, Ben," she said wearily. She hung up.

116

CHAPTER 21

April 29: Bluets

NOBODY EVER SHOWED up for town-planning-board meetings except the planning-board members themselves, those of the town's three welfare cases whose TV sets had broken down and left them without an evening's entertainment, and a few old people with hearing aids whose sons and daughters had convinced them that it would do them "good to get out of the house and meet people." (Actually, any good that was done was to the children themselves, who felt more comfortable with their porn videos or family fights or baby-making while the old folk were out.)

This evening's meeting included discussion of the Van Houten plan for the Oostdyk land behind Belding's. It had been assumed that the property had passed into the control of Billy Belding and that final decisions on the allowable extent of development could be arrived at. The chief issue was whether the thin, sloping soil would support the number of houses that Van Houten proposed, or if the various septic tanks would inevitably have a negative, if interesting, impact on neighboring wells. Van Houten was present, as were Harriet Lorimer and the Oostdyks. The local ecology group was represented by several of its officers with plans to further muddy the waters (so to speak) by raising the issue of visual pollution, by which was meant the covering of one of the highest points around with what amounted to a small town, visible for miles in every direction. Some university students were there as well, but mainly because, in the words of the old Groucho Marx ballad, "Whatever it is, I'm against it," especially if it was proposed by "the establishment," and even more especially if it involved an area many of them employed on weekends for camping and sundry biological experimentation unrelated to their studies.

So the crowd of over two dozen citizens in addition to the board itself was a record one, and an exercise in small-town American democracy was under way. The minutes of the meeting were incomplete; the recording secretary had been up all the previous night with her new baby and she felt it wiser to doze off from time to time rather than attempt to keep up with what was invariably not worth keeping up with, though usually presented at great length.

Among the highlights: A student rose and stroked an original composition on the guitar and sang the equally original lyrics that detailed at unbearable length her love for the open hills of Appleboro. There was no applause, an inaction in which the usually opposing factions present were for once in accord. A professor of economics offered projections of the tax revenues to be anticipated from several hundred new homes, as well as the increase in business for "support services" (stores, garages, service industries, etc.). He was neatly countered by another economist from the ecology group who estimated the outlays in increased town spending for roads, schools, police, and for the inevitable replacement of the volunteer fire department with full-time professionals.

A welfare recipient noisily departed his front-row-center seat, having concluded that watching a pictureless TV screen would be more entertaining, especially with a can of beer in hand, and a badly sprung easy chair more satisfactory than a folding chair that looked uncomfortably capable of continuing the folding process past the point of no return.

Then the moment of truth arrived: Van Houten's tame expert on soil management droned forth. He concluded that with maximum water usage by each dwelling, the underground aquifer was capable of supplying well over two hundred units for as far into the future as could be envisaged, and that the danger of overtaxing the drainage capacity of the soil was negligible, or, as he concluded dramatically, "indeed, for all practical purposes, absolutely nonexistent." He thumped a sheaf of papers as he uttered his last words, and the unexpected sound stirred the town recorder into wakefulness so that, somewhat resentfully, she was able to enter the proffered findings into the record.

"Are there any questions?" the chairman asked. There was silence. Van Houten smiled.

Harriet told herself that if no one else would—and no one ever did, at these meetings—she'd speak up. "Excuse me, sir," she said timidly, "but didn't you do the soil study on Mr. Van Houten's development near Asheville, in North Carolina?"

"That's right, ma'am. I did."

Harriet dug into her shopping bag and withdrew her own imposing sheaf of papers. "Well, I'm not an expert in these things, but if I'm reading this material I've got here correctly"—and she knew perfectly well she was reading it correctly—"there were several cases there where the waste water from one house drained into the wells of the houses next door. They finally decided the top layer of soil was too thin to absorb everything and it spread out all over the place. How can we be sure that isn't going to happen here?"

Van Houten took over from his expert. He smiled, attempting to project reassurance, but his teeth, to Harriet at least, looked pointier than normal. "That was nothing.

119

Simply several cases of faulty washing machines that didn't shut off properly and backed up into the water supply."

"You mean just soapy water backing up?" Harriet asked innocently. "Not the waste from the, ah, water closets?"

"That's it, little lady." Van Houten turned to the board and grinned, conveying the notion that the women-folk, bless 'em, should stay out of things they can't understand.

Which was what Harriet had been waiting for. Her voice lost its flutey tones and took on a more steely quality. "Really," she drawled, "that's terribly interesting. There were two cases of hepatitis down there, and they must be the first cases ever of hepatitis caused by soapy water."

"There's lots of ways a body can get hepatitis, lady."

"Right. And polluted water is one of them."

"Look, lady, you've heard the expert. You ought to stay out of things you don't understand."

"Don't you try kissing me off like that, Carl Van Houten. I demand that this board not take any action before we get an independent investigation. Why hasn't the Department of Environmental Conservation been called in?"

The chairman banged his gavel. "Order, please. I'm not sure this is a matter for the DEC."

"Yeah," someone shouted from the back, "of course, you're not sure. You'll be sure maybe only after you unload that swamp of yours down by the river on some poor sucker, huh?"

Harriet ignored the assist from the rear, which could have gotten the argument off on a tangent. "Well, then you can damn well find out who it *is* a matter for!" she said. "Who the hell does this board represent, Carl Van Houten or the people of Appleboro!"

Several people applauded, one of them a welfare case who appreciated a little action. A guitar was strummed in approval.

"Mrs. Lorimer," the chairman reproved, "you're out of order. The board is satisfied with the soil analyst's credentials, and we intend to act on the issue promptly. There's been enough time and taxpayer money spent on this already, going back for many months, and it's the function of the planning board to advance the business of the town, not hold it up indefinitely."

"Baloney!" a youthful voice hooted, trying to get back to the subject it had raised earlier. "And how much land you gonna sell Van Houten next, huh? You gonna let him have that Turtle Road swamp, stick a couple of hundred suckers with flooded basements, something like that, hey?"

Several people started talking at once, including the chairman, all trying to make themselves heard over the others. Harriet stood. "Wait!" she screamed, "Wait a minute! Please!" The room quieted down. "Mr. Chairman," she said, her voice deferential, "I'm not going to try to make any more speeches, but with your permission, I have a brief announcement of importance that bears on the subject of the meeting. May I?"

Pleased at having his authority once again recognized, the chairman nodded.

"It's just that everybody assumes something that really isn't true. I didn't want to say this, but there can't be any development up there on the hill because, as we all know, it needs a right-of-way across Jason Belding's land. I don't know how to tell it any way but straight out, but Jason left the decision to me in his will. To me, not to his son Billy. William, I mean."

"Are you saying you're the owner of the Belding place now, Mrs. Lorimer?" the chairman asked.

"No, not exactly. Jason Belding's grandchildren are the owners, but I'm the trustee, and nothing can be done with the land unless I say so. And I say, 'No.' So we can all go home." Harriet's voice was very soft, barely audible.

"Well, I'll be damned," Van Houten said angrily. "And you've just kept us dancing here while all along—"

121

He lost control. "Lady, you can just goddamned well kiss my butt, damn you!"

"Don't be so vague, young man." Harriet's voice took on volume again and descended into an alto register. "Be precise. That butt's pretty big. And while we're on the subject, why don't you put a couple of hundred houses on it instead? Lord knows there's lots of room." She turned and pushed out of the room, not confident that she would still have the last word if she hung around much longer.

Outside, she bent into the freshening wind as she headed for her car. The clouds were thickening; a storm was getting itself ready to blow. Storms inside and storms outside, she told herself as she squinted to peer into an infinity of gray slate boiling in the sky. She shuddered. I should have kept my fool mouth shut, she said silently. Once home, she turned the heat up high—high enough to make an Arab oil baron dance with delight—poured herself a stiff shot of brandy, and sat without the comfort of a lamp, looking out the window, staring without blinking and even without seeing. And still feeling cold.

Art Jessup was watching the approaching storm, as well. He yelled to Til in the bedroom that she had better start shutting any windows that were open. (Til always had too many windows open; she said a young boy like Bobby needed fresh air to grow strong and straight.) There was no response, no sound of windows going down.

"Til?" Jessup called. "You there?" He called into the rest of the house. "Til?" At this late hour, she couldn't be in the kitchen garden, but with Til these days you never knew. He opened the back door. A gust of wind blew icily into his face and he braced himself as he shouted, "Til! Where are you! Come on, get inside the house before the rain!"

Still no response. Grabbing a windbreaker off a peg, the man ran out to the barn. Til wasn't there. And neither, he saw to his alarm, was the pickup truck, which

Til hadn't driven for at least five years, since she had stopped going out, stopped doing everything except household chores and waiting for Bobby, waiting every minute of every blessed day, waiting to hear the boy drive up in his wreck of a jalopy to slam the door too hard and yell for his dinner. The car key was gone from its peg.

He turned around one way and then the other, really not knowing which way to turn, which way to go, and his glance fell on something else—an empty space, the space that should have held the gasoline can he had filled the other day so he could get the lawn mower going for the first cutting of the year. And he knew precisely where his wife had gone and what she was planning to do. He had to stop her.

Bobby's bicycle was leaning against a post. Til kept a sharp eye on it and made him keep it clean and oiled, and whenever the tires looked low, she nagged at him to pump them up. "The boy'll want to take a spin into town, soon's he gets a bite into that empty pit he uses for a stomach," she'd say, shaking her head fondly. Art wheeled the bicycle out and mounted it, heading into the wind. It was hard work for a man his age, a man who hadn't been on a bicycle for forty years, a man in his sixties, but it had to be done. She had to be stopped before she hurt herself. Before she hurt anyone else, either. He set off down the road, his knuckles white on the handlebars as he labored against the wind, against his aging muscles, against time, against his fears.

Harriet, still passively looking out her window, too tired to undress for bed, saw, in a sudden lightning flash, Art Jessup go past on a bicycle. The sight galvanized her; it made no sense. She stood and looked out for a better view and was able to make out a shape turning off the road and heading over the Belding place and up the hill. And she saw a dull red glow reflecting back from the clouds over the hill, clouds that were racing swiftly and trailing wisps

123

through the treetops as delicate and silent and ominous as the poisonous tentacles of a jellyfish.

While Harriet was struggling into a raincoat, Art Jessup reached the top of the rise. Everywhere there was flame; the frames for the few houses that Van Houten started before he knew there were to be problems with the land, several stacks of lumber, and a dead oak, destroyed by gypsy moths three years before, were crackling in the raging fire. Worst of all, the fire was tunneling under a millennium's accumulation of dead leaves, weeds, and debris, and wisps of smoke were rising as it burrowed forward rapidly.

"Til!" he shouted at the figure silhouetted against the blaze and running toward another pile of wood with a blazing rag on the end of a length of board. "Put that down, Til, put it down!"

The woman stopped abruptly and shouted, "No! Don't come any nearer. The devil Van Houten must be exorcised!" She waved her flaming brand like a woman of Salem marching on a witch at the stake. "Avarice is his god. 'His gold and silver is cankered and shall eat his flesh as it were fire!'"

She screamed as if the fires were within her own flesh, and she and Art advanced on one another. Somehow they both knew that this was mortal combat. With a sudden ferocious movement, Til swung her firebrand, and Art staggered back and fell into an open excavation, landing on a burning pyre of scraps and leaves and timber that workmen and wind and time had caused to accumulate.

The man shrieked, just one shrill cry, and the flames roared their furious welcome, reaching out to embrace the sacrifice their good fortune had brought. Til peered over the edge, and her face, lit from below by the consuming fire, resembled one of the evil demons she had thought to destroy. "Burn, devil," she whispered. "Burn. The fire will cleanse you of your sins." And she dropped her flaming stick down into the pit. "'Ashes to ashes!'" she shouted in triumph. Her words were punctuated by a tremendous thunderclap and the rain began in earnest.

Harriet arrived on the scene just as Jessup's body went over the edge to burn in the basement excavation. The waters poured down as if Til Jessup's personal god had elected, too late, to undo the deeds that had been done in his name. Harriet felt it soak through her rain gear and chill her flesh to ice, but the other woman ignored the elements to stand still as a long-dead tree trunk, gaunt and stripped of life, unaware of the world about her. Harriet made an instant decision: She could do nothing about Art, but she had better get the poor creature away from there and out of any further trouble as quickly as possible.

"Til, Til," Harriet called, "what are you doing out here! You're going to catch your death! Now let's get into your truck and back to my place to call the fire department. And get you into something dry. Come on, now." She took the woman by the hand and led her, unresisting, to the pickup. The key was in the ignition.

Someone had already called the fire department, and Harriet met them at the bottom of the hill. "I think it'll be all right," she yelled, "the rain's putting it out, but you better have a look. And I'm taking Mrs. Jessup here to my house. Please let Hugh Morrison at the state police station know, and tell him to get right over. It's important! Someone's up there! In the first excavation!"

Back at the house, Harriet led her passenger inside, unaware that the woman had reached for the carbine her husband kept under the seat for shooting game.

"There!" she said. "I'll get you some dry things and put on some tea. All right? Or would you like a little brandy? Do you good." She felt it would be important to sound cozy and reassuring if she was to get through to the woman.

Til was unresponsive. She stood stiffly in the hallway, just inside the door, unminding of her hair that had been plastered to her head by the torrent or of the drenched clothing that clung to her body. "I always liked you, Harriet Lorimer," she said dully, "always liked you. But why is my fire out? I heard. Are you a devil, too, Harriet Lorimer? Are you one of them, one of Carl Van Houten's crew? The fire was God's, God's fire to light and to put out as He saw fit. Not for you, it wasn't, woman. Not for you. I'll tell my husband. My Art will know what to do." Her head snapped up and she looked about. "Where is he, where is Art? Is he with my Bobby?"

"Now, Til," Harriet said gently, "I'm your friend. You know that."

"I know nothing anymore. I set the mountains on fire for the Lord. The Good Book says, 'A fire is kindled in mine anger, and shall set on fire the foundations of the mountains.'" She stared at Harriet. "I did the Lord's work. I set the mountains to blazing—and you put it out. I heard you." She lifted the carbine that had been at her side, concealed against her coat. "Fire cleanses."

Harriet's heart thumped. "Oh, Til. That's not fire. That's a gun. That's not what the Lord commands. He must do the judging, Til, not the two of us. That will anger the Lord." She groped in her memory for something to quote back. "Remember," she said, "the Good Book says we must be sure of the things we do; we must know before we act. 'Walk while ye have the light, for he that walketh in darkness knoweth not whither he goeth.' Remember that, my dear, and let the two of us sit down and seek the light." It was the only thing her racing heart would let her mind recall and she prayed that it would do the job.

Til frowned, uncertain. Others never quoted the Bible at her. She would have to think about that. She lowered the carbine and nodded. "We'll sit. We'll sit and you can pray. But the gun stays with me." She let Harriet lead her into the living room and they sat in the chairs that flanked the fireplace. Harriet hoped (and prayed) she looked devout, though she judged herself as most likely unconvincing. The other woman appeared satisfied, at least for the moment. Satisfied but wary.

They sat quietly for what may have been twenty minutes or may have been two hours; Harriet was unable to estimate. Til Jessup sat as if in a trance, unblinking, while her reluctant hostess, yearning for either that tea or the brandy she had so casually offered an eternity ago, sat equally still, not daring to break the spell and daring very little to hope. Only her eyes, as they studied the room, the walls, the furniture, the objects that might somehow assist in her release, betrayed any thought of action.

CHAPTER 22

April 29: Wild Azalea

MORRISON POUNDED ON the door. "Harriet, it's pouring out here! Come on, woman, let me in!"

Harriet looked hopefully at Til Jessup, but Til shook her head slowly from side to side. "I'm sorry, Mr. Morrison," she called, "but Mrs. Jessup is visiting and she'd rather not be disturbed." There was no response; Harriet knew that Hugh was trying to interpret her words. "She has something of Mr. Jessup's here and she's waiting for him to come over and get it." Desperately taking a chance, she added, "I think you call it a carbine or a thirty-thirty or something, and Mr. Jessup needs it for hunting. Mrs. Jessup has it in here for him."

Bob Pettit whispered to Morrison. "All the farmers, they've got carbines in their trucks. Anything they catch in the fields, they let 'em have it. First the old lady went nuts and killed her husband, and I bet you now she's pointing it at Mrs. Lorimer."

"You know these people. What the hell do we do?" Morrison whispered back, but Pettit spread his hands helplessly and remained silent. The rain was unremitting. Morrison wiped his running nose and cleared his throat.

128

"Yeah," he shouted. "I saw Mr. Jessup up the hill. He says you should give me the gun so I can take it to him, ma'am." There was no answer. "Mrs. Jessup?"

"I hear you clear, Policeman. You can't fool me with the devil's forked tongue. I stay here with my man's gun, and so does Harriet Lorimer."

Pettit whispered urgently. Morrison said to him, "Are you sure?"

"Hell, no, but it's all I can think of."

Harriet was in danger. If he did nothing, she'd stay in danger. If he took up Pettit's notion—God only knew what might bring the Jessup woman to the flash point. There was nothing fancy like a trained rescue squad or a smartass police psychologist in these parts. It was all on him to act or to wait, to get Harriet out or to put her life in even greater jeopardy.

He bit his tongue. "Mrs. Jessup. Art can't come now. He's going back home to see"—he looked helplessly at Pettit, who gave him the word he needed— "to see Bobby." Pettit whispered again. "Bobby's out of the army and he's back home again. Wants to see you." He waited. "Mrs. Jessup?"

"How do I know you're not lying to me? You're trying to trick me, aren't you? Well, it won't work. I stay here and this woman stays with me. You're a liar."

"Mrs. Jessup," Morrison said as softly as he could and still be heard above the storm. "God commands us to trust our neighbors. What does it say in Proverbs? 'The fear of man bringeth a snare, but"—Morrison and Til Jessup finished together—"whoso putteth his trust in the Lord shall be safe.'"

The woman's eyes focused on the room she was in, relinquishing her stare into some distant land. She turned toward Harriet and then toward the hallway. "Do you swear?"

"I swear."

"Will you take me to Bobby? To Art and Bobby?"

129

Pettit spoke softly into Morrison's ear. "I will," Morrison said, and promised himself someday if this ever ended, he'd take the woman to see her son's grave in the local cemetery. The shrinks would probably say it wouldn't do her any good—and as it turned out, it didn't—but it would do a world of good for him, Hugh Morrison, to let her see where her boy was lying.

The door opened and she went out, tight-lipped with suspicion. No one spoke. Morrison led her gently to the car, still without speaking. There was no time to see how Harriet was. "Go in and look after Mrs. Lorimer," he said to Bob Pettit. "Tell her I'll call, soon as I can." He drove off, and began wondering what would happen when Til Jessup realized she was going someplace that, whatever it was, wasn't home. Calling in on the car phone, talking cryptically, he managed to get the station to understand what to expect when he got there.

"It's a troubled world," he said to his passenger. "There are good people and evil people, aren't there? Hard to know what to do."

"Trust in God," Til said tersely. "Ask forgiveness."

They drove in silence. "Tell me, Mrs. Jessup, did you know Mr. Jason Belding?"

"I did."

"Did you know he was dead?"

"I did." She sat stiffly, as if hypnotised by the windshield wiper.

"Do you think he was an evil man? An evil man or a good one?" There was no answer. Morrison tried again, differently. "Do you think the wicked should die, Mrs. Jessup?"

"No. Not unless they spurn the Lord's mercy. 'If thou warn the wicked of his way to turn from it; if he do not turn from his way, he shall die in his iniquity.'"

"Did you punish Mr. Belding for his wickedness, Mrs. Jessup?"

She turned her head slowly and looked at her driver. "I'm not saying I did; I'm not saying I didn't."

"Did you warn him of his wickedness, the way the Bible says?"

"I tell you," she repeated, "I'm not saying I did; I'm not saying I didn't. 'Sufficient unto the day,' Mr. Policeman."

Morrison thought about the trouble with the land, Jessup's frustration over not selling out to Van Houten, about Belding's role in the long-running battle. He drew a deep breath and to himself he observed silently, I'm not saying you did, either, lady, and I'm not saying you didn't.

They drove on in silence, each occupied with his or her own dilemma.

Meanwhile, Harriet, badly shaken, watched her hands trembling, as if they were alien objects that had in some way become attached to her body. She shooed Bob Pettit out of the house, despite his objections, and poured herself an extravagantly large shot of single-malt scotch. She then drew a hot tub, hot as she could stand it, and climbed into it, clutching her drink. After she had settled down and felt the warm water spread its comfort through her body, and had willed her muscles to relax, she decided that this was where she just might take up permanent residence, never to get out again, once she could figure out how she might replenish the sustaining beverage from time to time.

CHAPTER 23

May 5: Bellwort

"**T**HEY'LL KEEP HER a while over at the state hospital," Morrison said. He picked gloomily at the green salad Harriet had put in front of him as phase one of her program to take a couple of inches off his waist. He wondered whether a corset might not have been less unbearable. "Damned grass. Couldn't you maybe crumble a little bacon in it?"

"No, I couldn't. But what about poor Til? I'm worried sick about her." She toyed with her own salad, not because her appetite was off but because she had taken the precaution of wolfing a peanut butter on whole wheat before Hugh showed up, wanting to set him an example by eating light.

"She doesn't really know what's happening to her. Keeps asking for Art and Bobby. I don't even think she's too unhappy. She's got a memory that goes back about two minutes. Anyway, it's you I'm worried about, Harriet. Why in the name of common sense did you have to announce to the whole damn world that anybody who wanted to put a road through the Belding land would have to deal with you first? It was crazy."

"I'm sorry. I was so furious with that smug toad of a

Carl Van Houten that I had to squash him. Anyway, the lawyer'll be back the end of the week and in a few days everybody will know what's in Jason's will no matter what I do."

"Yeah, but we need every minute we can get. Unless Til Jessup did it, there's a dangerous character running around loose, and he could have his sights set on you. He could figure you're the one in the way now. You've been real bad, kid." He stood. "And that's what I'm gonna be now, too."

"What?"

"Bad." He opened the refrigerator door and took out the bread, mayonnaise, and a package of ham.

Harriet sat passively. "At least put the mayo back. Make it mustard, Hugh."

He complied. "Listen. Why don't you go take a trip for a week or two. Get one of your girl friends to go drive down to Washington, go to the museums down there. It's pretty there in the spring. And maybe Williamsburg, grab yourself a little history. What do you say?"

"You know what I say." She looked annoyed. "Not till this is settled."

"Nothing you can do here, you know."

"Let me try, Hugh." She raised a hand before his protest came out. "I mean, after all, I know so much about Jason that I don't even know how much I know. Please. Take me up to his place and let me look around. Maybe I'll see something. Look," she said, seeing Morrison's doubtful expression, "what harm can it do?"

"I'll think about it." He bit his sandwich hard, as if subduing it. "Let you know."

Harriet knew she had won. She turned her thoughts to another aspect of her upset. "Hugh," she said, "I don't know what's happening to Appleboro. People are getting ugly. It's as if this awful thing has poisoned the air and we're all succumbing."

"What's the trouble? I knew there was something

bothering you, but I figured if you wanted to say it, you'd say it."

"Maybe I'm exaggerating. Maybe it's just Ben Stoddard, but he's never been so ugly before. Catty I'm used to, but he's gotten so vicious. He called me a couple of days ago and I swear the only reason was so he could say that Henry Oostdyk and Elfie had had an affair. Something sordid, the way he made it sound. Motel rooms."

Morrison burst out laughing. "That little librarian in a motel room? Your boy Stoddard has a great imagination. I'd bet they were pasting stamps in an album, if that much." He slapped his thigh and snorted again.

Harriet tossed a piece of lettuce, which had dressing on it, at the man. It landed on his necktie, where it did no discernible extra damage. "Oh, shut up, you sexist pig. This was supposed to be years ago, before Henry and Judith. I'm glad you enjoy it."

"Me, too. Hey, you don't suppose it's true, do you?"

"It could be, I guess, but I wouldn't know. That was before I lived up here full-time, and I wasn't much up on the local dirt. I know we'd see Henry and Elfie together back then." She glared. "And she was a pretty little thing, too, Hugh Morrison. Not overweight, like some I might mention."

Morrison's shoulders shook with renewed relish at the mental picture he had formed of the long-ago sweethearts. "I'm sorry. I can't help it. You took me by surprise. Anyway, you've given me an idea. I think I'll have a little talk with our Mr. Stoddard; maybe he'll be a little more open now."

"Oh, Hugh! You won't give me away, will you?"

"My lips are sealed."

"Well, then, if you're going to see the man, there's another thing you might want to know. He's fishing around for something—I don't know what—about black stars. You know, a not-too-expensive gemstone. Some kind of story about a gift for a niece." She recounted the telephone call

134

from Ben. "And Jason and Betty had these black stars, and I just know, I'm positive, Ben Stoddard is cooking up some kind of trouble for somebody."

"Good. That's the kind of help I need from you. Look, I've got to be on my way now. Thanks for the new-mown hay."

"Hey, wait a minute. What about my going up to Jason's?"

"I'll be in touch." He left.

Ed and Virginia Lorimer were in their living room in Manhattan after dinner. The news had just ended on TV and Virginia was putting dinner on the table. Ed walked in to help. "You know, honey," he said, "I'm worried about Mother. Judith Oostdyk called me at the office today. She said they're worried about her, too. People up there figure now that Mother's the one standing in the way of this lousy housing development, if anybody's going to be in danger, it'll be Ma."

"What can you do about it? Now don't get too smart."

"I thought I'd give her a call, ask her to come down for a spell. Get her away from there."

"Sweetheart, I'd love to have her, but there's no room!"

"I know, but I'll be off in Atlanta to see a client and I figured maybe you'd like to go with me, take a little vacation. Mother'd love to take care of the kids. She'd get a real charge out of it. Just for Friday and the weekend."

Virginia looked doubtful. "You could try, but if she gets the idea you're treating her like an old lady who has to be looked after, she'll explode. Go ahead and call, but for heaven's sake be careful!"

"Don't worry, I will. I'll try now." He dialed. "Hello, Ma? How's it going? Everything okay? Gypsy moths coming back this year?" His voice boomed with good cheer. After a few minutes of gossip, he said, "Listen, Ma, I've got to go off to Atlanta and I'd like to take Vir-

135

ginia with me, give the girl a couple of days off, like. Friday till Monday morning. How'd you like to take care of the kids for us? They're in a good phase, thank God, though Lord knows how long that may last, and we thought you might get a kick out of it."

"Why, I'd love to, Ed."

"Great! When can you get here?"

"Oh, Ed, that's foolish. Why don't you bring them up here, let them have the open country to play in. It's gorgeous here now. The trees are getting green; the wild flowers are up. You know how you used to love it yourself. Put them on the bus and I'll pick them up at the station."

"Well, Ma, we thought you'd maybe like to come down to the city instead. Have a little vacation for yourself. A couple of shows, museums, maybe the stores. You know."

Harriet was incredulous. "With the kids?" she asked. "Why, I'd just be boxed into that apartment of yours. You know that. How in the world— Hey, wait a minute, you've been talking to somebody in Appleboro, haven't you? Or maybe you got the story from Billy Belding. And you think you'll take poor helpless old granny off the scene before she gets herself in trouble. Well?"

"Ma, be reasonable. You've got yourself in a pretty tight spot, and Virginia and I thought you ought to duck out for while, until the police find out what's going on."

"Well, think again. I've got a job to do here and I'm not going to stop until I find out who's responsible for Jason's death, who killed my dearest friend. And if you think it's any lure for me to go to New York and spend an eternity in an apartment with the kids, you're crazy. Look, I love the babies, but I've done all that and now it's your turn. I don't really ever want to scrape peanut butter off a floor again; I'm bored with cracker boxes clawed apart over the label reading OPEN OTHER END; I can live perfectly well without shutting all the drawers and cabinets in a kitchen eighty times a day, and if you like, I can go on with this indefinitely."

"Not necessary, Ma. I get the idea."

"Very well. You want to send the kids up here, I'd love to have them. But I'm not going down there to hide in your broom closet for the duration. Capeesh, boy?"

"Yes, Ma."

After they said goodbye and hung up, Virginia Lorimer said to her husband, "You know, Ed, you sounded about ten years old when you said 'Yes, Ma.'"

"That can't be. I didn't feel a day over seven."

Pinky looked up when Morrison got back to the station house. "Hey, Hugh, you got a call from the Oostdyk woman. Says would you give her a buzz when you get a chance."

"Right. Thanks. And a little advice, buddy. Don't let that one hear you calling her the Oostdyk woman. She'll give *you* a buzz you won't forget."

"Next time I date the broad, I'll keep it in mind."

Morrison pulled the phone across his desk, causing a sheaf of new reports from headquarters to flutter to the floor. He grunted as he scooped them up; he wondered whether medical science was, as usual, wrong, and whether these slops Harriet was feeding him were ending up on the old waistline fast as ice cream. "I'd like to speak to Mrs. Oostdyk. Senior Investigator Morrison calling."

"This is she. Thank you for returning my call. I've got something I'm sure is Jason Belding's, and I think you ought to have it."

"Yes, ma'am. What is it you've got?"

"A key chain, actually. Set with a little black gemstone."

"Be right out, ma'am."

At the Oostdyk house, Judith produced the key ring. "I'm quite sure it has no particular value, but I thought you should have it."

"You're right, and thank you. Where did you get it, Mrs. Oostdyk?"

"Actually, I feel like a fool, because I've had it ever

137

so long and simply forgot about it. I was out walking when the snows started to clear off the fields and I simply found it. Sometime in March. And, of course, since no one knew anything was wrong with Mr. Belding, I dropped it in a bureau drawer to wait until he got home from Florida. And then I forgot. Stupid of me, but I simply forgot."

"That's understandable. Whereabouts did you find it?"

"I can probably take you to the exact spot, oh, about fifty feet in from the road near the middle school. You know, the open field just past the school as you go out Freddies Lane toward Kingston. Oh, I think it's Chestnut Hill Lane since they put the name changes in."

"Yeah, I know what you mean. I don't think we need the exact spot right now. I'll let you know if we do. And again, I appreciate this. Thanks, Mrs. Oostdyk."

"Not at all."

Later on, the man called Harriet. "Listen, girl, is your friend Ben Stoddard the kind who would creep into somebody's bedroom, go through the bureau drawers?"

"Oh, I doubt it. He's too chicken for that. He'll nose through your whole kitchen and run barefoot through the medicine chest, and if there's a silver drawer in your dining table, he'd probably crawl in, but I'm sure he wouldn't dare wander through anybody's unmentionables. Too tricky. Too dangerous."

"That's what I figured. And tell me, your Mrs. Oostdyk doesn't look like much of an outdoor girl to me. She likely to go hiking around the fields at the edge of town?"

"Judith? You've got to be kidding! She's the type takes the car to the mailbox at the foot of the drive. Listen, if she had the money and the nerve, she'd hire a sedan chair to take her to the supermarket, plus native boys to wag the groceries back home behind her, single file, like a safari."

"I figured that, too. Thanks, Harriet, you're more help than you know."

"Well tell me, then. I'd like to know."

"Some other time, maybe."

Later, when he estimated Stoddard would be home from the school, Morrison called the man. "Mr. Stoddard, this is Senior Investigator Morrison. I'd like to drop over and talk to you. No, it won't take long. No, tomorrow won't do. I'm afraid it'll have to be right now. Yes, a matter of some urgency. Okay, I'll be there in five minutes."

Whether Ben Stoddard was married, divorced, deserted, or single, his home was nevertheless the abode of a lonely and uncommitted cipher. Nothing looked personal. The pictures on the living room wall were reproductions of the less unsettling works of Van Gogh, a Gainsborough Blue Boy, and one of Mr. Audubon's pretty birdies. A faded length of beige carpeting covered the center of the floor, complementing the washed-out ambience of the room, and the only sense of life that Morrison could discern was centered about an excessively undusted imitation Tiffany lamp by the side of a squat and characterless easy chair. The place looked like a cheap hotel room, impersonal and shoddy.

Morrison sailed, uninvited, into the easy chair—the one that clearly proclaimed itself as the lord of the manor's personal and private throne—the better to put his host at his unease. "Now, Mr. Stoddard, I won't beat around the bush," he said brusquely. "Are you sure you can't remember anything about Jason Belding you'd like to tell me?"

"There's nothing more I can say about the dear man. I've told you everything I know."

"It's been my impression, sir, that you've told me all the gossip you know but damn few of the facts."

"I can't imagine what you mean. And I can't say I care for your attitude." Stoddard sat up straight and in attempting to look fierce succeeded only in resembling a caricature of an English butler who has heard an interloper in the town house break wind.

"Have you ever heard the phrase 'obstruction of justice?' 'Aiding and abetting a criminal?' Anything like that?" Stoddard remained silent. "You may learn about them yet. You and I both know, Mr. Stoddard, that there's a lot you haven't told me. To begin with, there's the matter of a black-star gemstone that you found. For starters, you can tell me about that. And before you begin, Mr. Stoddard, may I remind you that keeping knowledge of anything like this all to yourself is one of the best ways in the world to commit suicide." (The words *Mr. Stoddard* were beginning to sound like a curse.)

"What's that supposed to mean?"

"Only that there's somebody in this town who might want to make sure you didn't get a chance to tell the police too much. You've hinted to everybody in a five-mile radius that there's something you know, and you'll either tell me about it now or I'll have to take you in. Which might be a good idea anyway, just to keep you out of danger."

Stoddard turned white. Morrison wondered if he was going to gallop off to get his smelling salts, but instead he said, "Well, do I have your word that this is confidential?"

"You have no word at all from me, sir. If everyone knows you're aware of the black star and if they all know you've snooped through every house in town, how can anything be confidential?"

The man blushed and squirmed on his seat. "It's this way," he finally said in defeat. "You see, I was visiting Mrs. Oostdyk and I felt this splitting headache coming on. I went to the medicine cabinet for an aspirin, and all I did was open it up and there was this stone, black with a star in it, sitting on the shelf. I had no idea what it was. That's all there is to it."

"No, you had no idea, but you found out later, didn't you?"

"As a matter of fact, just in conversation I learned

that Jason Belding had a couple of black stars." A wave of false courage swept over the man and he lashed out, or at any rate thought he was lashing out. "I suppose your new dear friend Mrs. Lorimer tells you all about these things. Tells you everything, I'd guess, just like she used to with Jason Belding."

"Mr. Stoddard, I am a police officer. I have to keep my personal feelings out of my work, so I'll let that pass." (To himself, he added: "How would you like a fat lip, Mr. Stoddard, sir?") "Now let's stick to the facts. You say you saw this black star in a medicine cabinet." Stoddard nodded. "Are you sure you didn't go rummaging through any other part of the house to see what you could find, like a lady's bureau? This is important. Your life may depend on it."

"Certainly not. I'm not a snoop, nor am I a thief."

"Yeah, that's great. Where is that stone now? Did you take it?"

"I told you! Never! I put it right back where I found it."

"Okay. Tell me why, since you knew or found out that this was Jason Belding's, why didn't you tell the police about it? It's clear you suspected some connection between finding it in the Oostdyk house and the murder of Jason Belding, but you decided not to cooperate with the police. Isn't that right?"

"One doesn't lightly accuse one's friends of murder on the basis of a piece of polished rock of no particular value."

"I suppose not. But one's friends, if they include a murderer, might not extend the same courtesy to you, sir. Have you thought about that, Mr. Stoddard?" Morrison rose from the easy chair. "If there's anything else you'd like to tell me"—Stoddard shook his head—"you know where to find me. And Mr. Stoddard."

"Yes?"

"Look under your bed tonight before you turn in."

141

CHAPTER 24

May 6: Clover

ELSA NEISWENDER, SECRETARY, assistant, and general factotum to J. L. McCollum, principal of the grade school, was seated on a high stool in her office, working on the slant-top artist's table she used to prepare the bulletin sent out to the parents once a term. Miss Neiswender was a sensible woman of forty-six and a good worker, but her trim figure, pale and poreless skin dramatized by raven-black hair, and full petulant lips, gave her an air of smouldering abandon. Every ten-year-old boy in the school, plus his older brother and in some cases even his father in his time, had stood next to her desk and attempted, with conspicuous failure, to peer down the forbidden depths of her blouse. Following such boldness, the boy would invariably report back to his peers that he had "seen it all," whatever "all" might have meant to him.

At the moment, Miss Neiswender was drawing a picture of a basketball hoop on top of the sports column when the boss came in. J. L. was fat and persistent and smelled stale. Miss Neiswender pressed her lips together grimly.

"Ah, Elsa," the boss said, "working on the bulletin? Good!" He walked over and peered across her shoul-

142

der. "Maybe that line should be a shade darker, you think?" He leaned across to point and as he did so, managed to press against her upper arm a part of his anatomy that would more properly have been left for pressing against his wife's upper arm.

Miss Neiswender gritted her teeth. Three years ago, she had filed a complaint with the school board, but J. L. had gotten to them. The good ole boys had stuck together. The chairman had called her in and explained that they sympathized with the difficulties many ladies experienced while they were going through the change of life, and that they were willing to overlook such behavior of hers as might have been caused by emotional upset. "Temporary" emotional upset, the bastard had added. If she went back again now, they'd either decide she was going through the longest menopausal agony on record or else just call her a liar.

"Tell me, Elsa, has Mr. Stoddard called in sick? He didn't show up for his classes and it's not like him to fail to let us know. I'm a little concerned." He emphasized his little concern by pushing it against Miss Neiswender's arm again, just for a moment.

"No, Mr. McCollum. At least, I haven't heard." The phone rang over at her desk. "Oh, I'll get that!" she said. She spun around rapidly and with her elbow managed to land a wicked jab in the boss's groin. She continued her rapid course toward the phone.

"Hello, Mr. McCollum's office." She gazed happily at the doubled-over man clutching himself below the waist. "I'm sorry, but Mr. McCollum is overwhelmed at present and he couldn't possibly. Try us again this afternoon. You're welcome."

"Oh, Mr. McCollum," she gasped, "do you feel ill? Can I help?"

"No, Elsa," he grunted, "I'll go back and rest a while. It'll be okay." Still in obvious pain, hunched forward, he exited, not exactly walking and not exactly per-

143

forming what might have been mistaken for an aboriginal dance of major ceremonial import.

Miss Neiswender picked up her phone. "Hello, Beverly? Listen, I took your advice. Yeah. I let old Lover Nuts have it. No, not with my foot, stupid, with the elbow. An accident, you know? So what do you think about going out for dinner tonight? I feel like celebrating. I'll fix Momma something, meet you about six-thirty at the Wicky Wacky for drinks, and we'll take it from there. I can taste that steak already!"

CHAPTER 25

May 8: Forking Catchfly

THE SHOPRITE MALL was the Appleboro equivalent of the ancient Athenian agora, the small-town meeting place dreamed of by Thomas Jefferson in his hopes for a democratic America. The bank, the Oostdyk bank, was in the mall, together with the supermarket, the movie house, the hardware store, and a general store that called itself a junior department store, meaning that anything a citizen might require more exotic than a muffin tin was unavailable. In season, the flea-market benefit for the Reform church was held there, though the local Catholic church, St. Sebastian's, staged its own parallel affair in their meeting hall when a night not reserved for Bingo could be isolated. To the despair of Appleboro gentry, the local restaurant, the Huguenot Manor, was down West Chestnut Street a fair piece, and as a result, the fast-food outlet in the mall, with its odor of stale grease, was strategically placed to make serious inroads into the lovelier world of relish trays, blueberry muffins, lamb stews, and pumpkin pies.

The only serious commercial enterprise besides the restaurant not in the mall was the local antique shop. A marketing instructor at the nearby university in New Paltz had determined by survey that most of the customers were wide-eyed innocents from New York City lusting after the rusted iron skillets, the cracked mugs, and the glass milk bottles that Appleboro housewives had finally decided to chuck out, and that a less modern setting would be more productive for the larcenous machinations of an antique dealer.

So it was inevitable that Harriet Lorimer and Judith Oostdyk would run into each other while grocery shopping. Each peered into the other's shopping cart to see what was going to be on the stove this week, whether the vegetables were fresh, frozen, or canned, and whether there was any possibility of gathering dirt to be dished later on such topics as who was using a shameful amount of precooked frozen dinners instead of doing it from scratch, and who was stocking up on the dented canned goods that were marked down by as much as 50 percent.

"Harriet, dear," Judith oozed, "it's been too long! We haven't gotten together since—why, it's been since the last time you were over for bridge, hasn't it?"

"I know. It's awful of us both. I don't know where the time goes. And I suppose I haven't felt too much like going out these days. Every time I do, I think I should be doing it with Jason. . . ." Her voice trailed off.

Impulsively, Judith put a hand on Harriet's arm. "Oh, Harriet, I'm so sorry. You poor sweet. But we've got to keep going, don't we!"

"Don't you worry about me. I'll never quite get over it, but I'll be dancing on the piano again. Don't you worry about that." Nervously, Harriet felt a need to change the subject; sympathy could be more distressing than the pain it was designed, however sincerely, to alleviate. "And what have you been up to? Keeping busy, I'll bet." She laughed. "How many new boards are you chairing since we saw each other last, ten?"

Judith looked earnest. "Actually, Harriet, I haven't

146

been doing so much lately. Let's sit a moment over here in the sun. I've been wanting to talk to you about that, as a matter of fact."

Harriet wondered whether she was going to be dragooned into volunteer work, which she couldn't abide, or into a contribution to Judith's latest cause, which she couldn't afford. Of the two, she'd prefer the contribution, putting it down to having bought her way out of something she felt ill-equipped to wrestle with. The ladies sat themselves in the sun on a stone and wooden bench whose plaque advised that it commemorated Josiah and Rebecca Janvier and that it had been donated to the people of Appleboro by their great-granddaughter Judith Janvier Oostdyk and her husband Henry Oostdyk.

"Now, Harriet, dear, I don't know how to begin except by beginning, so let me say that I know how much this little town means to you, almost as much as to those of us whose people came here three hundred years ago."

Harriet pondered the likelihood that after three hundred years the town might mean ten times as much as it did to someone who had only had thirty years' worth of local roots. She knew she wasn't going to like this, but she held her peace. "Yes, it does."

"And it took a great deal of courage to do what you did the other night at the town meeting, announcing right out that you were in charge of Jason's property and you weren't going to let that dreadful Carl Van Houten have access to the land behind it."

"That's right, and I meant it."

"I don't doubt that you did, and that's what I want to talk to you about. This is embarrassing, but without boasting, I think can fairly say that Henry and I have done a lot for Appleboro." Harriet nodded her agreement. "The library, the hospital, the park, the swimming pool—they're just the visible things. But you know that as well as I do. And frankly, it's a matter of balancing one thing against another. We may not like what Van Houten does to the land, but it'll give us money to keep helping, to do the things that our people have done for Appleboro over the years. One small section of town will be, how can I put it, uglified" (she giggled unhappily) "but in the long run we'll all benefit. Don't you see?"

Harriet drew a deep breath. "I'm sorry, Judith, but I don't. It isn't as simple as Carl Van Houten blighting the landscape with too many houses. It's much worse than that. The land just can't support all that building. There's not enough well water and the soil is too thin for proper drainage. Van Houten's got a terrible reputation for putting up these disasters and then running out."

"But the town board has looked into it, and they're satisfied. Surely they understand the problem better than we do!"

"Surely they do. And equally surely the board members have land of their own they want to sell. I'm sorry for the old farmers who have nothing now but their land, and who want to sell out now that prices are up, but there's got to be a better way than turning the place into a typical overbuilt, deadly suburban crush. And that's just what will happen. If Van Houten crams his houses onto your property, don't you think poor Art Jessup had just as much right as the Oostdyks to expect to sell to someone else who wants to put up a rural slum in place of the corn and the hay fields, a quarter or a half acre to each lot?"

"But that's different! People like the Jessups would take the money and be off to Florida or someplace like that. The money Henry and I get will be ploughed right back into Appleboro. We have an obligation to keep the town livable, Henry and I. But it takes money, more money than we can manage right now. This is our hometown and it needs us to take care of it properly. We love it; we understand it. If that land behind Jason is lost, we know how to make it up to the town in a thousand ways. Our people have been here for hundreds of years, and, Harriet, we *are* the town, don't you see?"

148

Back and forth a few more times, the ladies not talking to each other so much as past each other, and Harriet had had enough. She knew she was going to say things she would be sorry for, but she didn't know, or want to know, what choice she had. "Judith," she said firmly, "I don't see any point in going on with this. You keep telling me about managing this and managing that. And that you and Henry are the town; you know the town. All right, you love the place. So do I. So do many others who live here. Maybe we even love it more because we sought it out; we chose it consciously."

Judith started to interrupt, but Harriet said, "No, wait a minute. Let me finish. Others know this town as well as you do. Others work to help the town and are even willing to do more. To put it bluntly, Judith, you have every right to be proud that your people have been here for three hundred years, but you have no right at all to be vain about it or to think that that gives you some sort of special wisdom or to act as if you were nursemaid for a collection of cuddly but incompetent children. Look, some of the Jessup cows have been on the land that long, too, banging out calves over the centuries, and as far as that goes, the only difference between them and the Oostdyks and the Janviers is that you people did the banging out in four-posters, while the cows used the barn. Now let's have no more of this. To put it bluntly, the constant rape of the land that goes on around here is sinful, literally immoral, and you are not going to change my mind. That's final."

Judith's voice grew ominously cool. "Harriet," she said quietly, almost sweetly, "do you have any land around here apart from your home?"

Harriet knew the woman was up to something but couldn't figure out what. There was no option other than a straight answer. "No, I don't, as you know perfectly well. Why?"

"No reason, really. I was just thinking. Neither, it seems to me, do any of the other people, the ecology nuts and the rest of them wringing their hands and telling me and other people of substance what's right and what's wrong, what we can and can't do with our property. It's so easy for people with no responsibilities in this world to set themselves up as judge and jury and lecture everybody else on what's moral and what isn't." She bristled.

"All right, Judith. What are you getting at? Let's have it."

"Nothing much. Only that it occurs to me that it's awfully easy to be sure what's moral and immoral when it's not going to cost you anything yourself. Put simply, my dear"—and here her voice took on an oratorical tone—"I'd say that morality is all too often the last refuge of the failure. Goodbye." With that she turned and walked off, head held high, showing Harriet only her ample back.

I'll be damned, Harriet thought. Not only is Judith Oostdyk getting to look more like Oscar Wilde every day, but now she's even beginning to sound like him!

CHAPTER 26

May 10: Yellow Goat's-Beard

"COME ON, HUGH," Pinky protested, his swivel chair squeaking as he shifted position to face Morrison. "It looks like old lady Oostdyk agrees with me. She figures her husband knocked off this Belding guy, and after your little Mr. Stoddard finds this fancy key ring in the medicine cabinet, she decides to head him off at the pass. She tells you she found it like under a cabbage leaf or in the oysters Rockefeller way back before anybody knew there was anything wrong, and then she forgot about it. So now she remembers, she says, and she wants you to have it. What she means is, she wants to get her story in before this big mouth Stoddard tells his. Protect her old man. Simple."

"Yeah?" Morrison asked. "Maybe, but I still don't like it. First place, Henry Oostdyk's got a good alibi for during the day when Belding was murdered. And I don't think he'd be likely to tempt anybody into taking a walk in the fields at night around here, not on December fifth last year, anyway. I checked, and it was sleeting, thermometer below freezing."

"What the hell, he could have thought of some-

151

thing, get the man out of his house, go for a walk, take a look at that right-of-way, smash his head in."

"Sure he could have. You're right. Then he takes this black-star thing. What for, a souvenir? Puts it on the shelf of the medicine cabinet, where he keeps all his jewelry?" He shook his head. "I don't like it."

"Got any better ideas?"

"No."

"Then, boy, you need another suspect. This Belding and your Van Houten got pretty solid stories how they couldn't've done it. Especially Van Houten. How about the Jessup woman? She could've got the man mixed up with the Great Satan and ten minutes later she could've forgotten, maybe thought she just baked a coconut-cream pie."

"You think you're kidding, Pinky, but it could've been like that. In her crazy way, she figured the land and Van Houten and her son not being home were all mixed up together. You know the poor woman still can't accept it, that her husband isn't coming home anymore? I hope that's not the answer. But it could've been," he repeated. "It could've been."

"So now?"

"So now I'm going back up to the Belding place, look around. Harriet Lorimer's been bugging me to take her up there, let her take a shot at it. Maybe she'll spot something we missed. What the hell. What's to lose?"

Not, Pinky thought, your innocence, but somehow he figured it might be smart to leave the words unsaid.

"George," the postmaster said, "Bobby Kerr was in this morning saying how his pension check is three days late, wondering if you put it in the wrong box again. Who's got the box next to his?"

The answer came back, "On the right, it's Kelly. Stoddard to the left. Want I should look?"

"Yeah. I hope to God it's not in Stoddard's box. That son of a bitch opens everything he can get his hands on, then tells me he's so sorry, he didn't know it was for somebody else."

Dolly looked up from her sorting mail in the back room and called out, "Hey, why don't we get the old snoop a rubber stamp, 'Opened by mistake,' let him have it for Christmas?" The three of them laughed.

"It's not in Kelly," George announced.

"Oh, God, don't let it be in Stoddard."

"Not in Stoddard, either. But you know what? Stoddard's box is jammed full. Looks to me like he hasn't been in to pick up in a while, maybe."

"That's not like him."

"Think anything's wrong?"

"I don't know. Probably not. Who's driving that route this week? Ask them to take a look at his box out on the road, see if he's been clearing that out, okay?"

"Roger, wilco." George was in the National Guard and given to military expressions, not entirely unaware of how much this annoyed the postmaster, who had been too young for Korea and wasn't tagged for Vietnam and thought the National Guard was an elaborate plot to get days off for his staff that couldn't be counted against their vacation time.

Harriet grabbed Morrison's arm to steady herself as they walked up the rise to Jason's house. The daffodils, sturdy beasts that took care of themselves regardless of late freezes, rain, drought, and the predations of the hordes of nearly tame deer that roamed the countryside, were well up. The early ones had even died back. Sadly, she pinched off a few seed heads so the bulbs would save their strength for flowering next year; Jason, in his methodical way, would have been doing this.

The lawn was an overgrown disaster. "Hugh, would it be all right if I had the lawn mowed. It's so depressing as it is, I can't look at it. You don't need it left like this, do you?"

"No, go ahead. You'd think the son would see to that, wouldn't you?"

Harriet didn't respond. They went up to the front door in silence and Morrison unlocked it. "Okay, old girl, take a look. We're finished, so don't worry about upsetting things."

Not knowing what she was looking for, Harriet traced a finger sadly through the dust on the table Jason used as a desk. The calendar was still open to December 5. In his usual methodical way, Jason had written down whatever he had wanted to accomplish that last day—take the cat to the farm, unplug the television set, turn off the pump. He had even put down "Airport bus 9 P.M.," as if he could have forgotten. Harriet's lower lip trembled in spite of herself.

She looked at the neatly arranged pillows on the sofa, the handful of phonograph records, the smaller collection of video tapes, all carefully labeled with the names of the programs that Jason had taped and decided to keep rather than to erase in favor of another taping. More precisely, she had done the taping herself, coming over to set up the machine, which Jason proclaimed himself incapable of doing on his own, and for which she charged, according to the time of day, either a glass of wine, a double vodka martini on the rocks, or a large cognac in a balloon snifter. Then, on rising the next day, Jason would rewind the tape—this he was able to do without help—and remove it, always reminding Harriet, if she was there, that she should do the same with her own tapes, since if they remained partly unwound for too long, they tended to stretch out of shape. Or so he had read somewhere. Such memories, inconsequential but dear, flooded in on her.

She sat down and sighed. Only the day before, December 4, she had been over at lunchtime and set the machine up for taping an old Dietrich movie that was coming on in the early-morning hours, a movie Jason had seen over forty years ago and that he had remembered fondly.

Harriet had warned him not to try to look at it again, but he had been adamant. He'd never see it now, and in fact, she noted that he hadn't even had the chance to rewind, remove, label, and put it on his shelf. Sadly, almost mechanically, she turned the VCR on and went through the rewinding procedure herself.

Succeeding in keeping her voice steady, she said, "I don't see anything here, Hugh. Let's go through the rest of the house." In the bedroom, they looked at Jason's little box of cuff links, collar stays, and two old class rings. Harriet picked up one earring, a black star. "This was Betty's," she explained. "Jason had the other one reset as a key ring. He never put a key on it, but he liked to have it with him, even though it dug holes in his pockets. God knows where it is now."

God and Morrison both knew, but neither spoke out.

The kitchen was tidy except for the inevitable and ubiquitous layer of dust. Morrison waved a hand in the direction of the garbage pail. "That's where the son found the cat. I guess the poor thing knew where the garbage was kept and she tried to rassle up something to eat."

"What do you mean, that's where Billy found the cat? What happened to the animal?"

"I thought you knew. After—after it happened, the cat was alone here, nothing to eat. Before your friend was able to get it to someone to take care of."

"Oh, poor Jezebel. Jason loved that animal. They had cocktails together every night, Jason used to say, before he put her out."

"He put the cat out? All winter, in this climate?"

"Well, sort of. Not exactly out. In the daytime, he let her in or out as she pleased, but at night, he put her in the garage. The furnace is in there, so it never gets cold, and there's one of these pet ports in the garage door. You know? A little opening she could use to get out and back in again when she wanted to do her business. Jason refused to

155

have anything to do with kitty-litter pans, so he fed her at five, when he'd have an evening drink—that was their cocktail hour together, Jason and Jezebel. Then he'd put her in the garage, let her in again the next morning."

"Always? Did he ever vary the routine? Not put her out?"

"Jason? Jason vary a routine?" A gentle smile creased Harriet's face. "Never. Besides, do you see a litter pan anywhere in the house? No, he couldn't have let Jezebel stay inside."

"And always at five?"

"Always. Drinks and cat food at five, Jezebel out at five-thirty, another drink for Jason until six. Then he'd turn on the TV news, fix his dinner, go back and forth from the TV set to the kitchen, and sit down to eat at seven-thirty, when the national news was over."

"Why didn't you tell me this before?"

"Well, I like that! You never let me up here before; you never told me about Jezebel. Does it matter?"

"Sure it matters. It means he was killed before the cat went out, before five, five-thirty."

"Is that important?"

"Anything that narrows things down is important. Besides—" He stopped.

"Besides, what?"

"Nothing, I guess. Something else I thought of, that's all." He decided he had no right to say that murder before five took Henry Oostdyk a little further off the hook, since he was in the bank all day on December 5. If he hadn't said the Oostdyk man was on the hook, there was no point in saying he was now more or less off it. And Harriet Lorimer, after all, was a civilian, not a police officer.

Morrison drew a deep breath. It was all very well to clear a suspect. That wasn't the problem. The problem was finding a replacement.

156

"I tell you, there's something wrong up there and I'd hate to say what it was!" The man on Rural Route 2 leaned over nearer the postmaster and treated him to a sampling of lunchtime garlic. "Stoddard's box was crammed, so I went up the drive to the house. Knocked on the door, no answer. Looked through a couple of windows."

"And?" the postmaster asked. "See anything?"

"Well, no, not exactly," the route man said reluctantly. "But I tell you, I got a whiff of this sweet smell, sort of a rotten smell, like when there's a dead woodchuck or something on the road too long!"

The postmaster looked around nervously. "For God's sake, keep your voice down! First place, you've been reading too many mystery books. Anything wrong in that house, you're not going to be smelling it through the windows."

"Now wait a minute, I tell you—"

"Second place, you want to set Dolly off again? You just do that, you'll be damned sorry, let me tell you. Last year you come in with that story about a dead deer smeared to hell and gone on Route 44 and you know what happened; Dolly started puking all over the lousy place. Took us half a day to sponge off the Christmas mail. So keep your trap shut, will you!"

"Yeah, okay. Have it your way. You're the boss. But something's wrong up at Stoddard's. Mail settin' out there, box all crammed."

"Okay, okay. Just keep it quiet. I'll take it from here. We'll let Bob Pettit have this one. His job, not ours." He picked up the phone and dialed the police station, cupping the mouthpiece to keep his voice from drifting out to Dolly. "Hello, Bob? Smitty here. Yeah, over at the post office. Listen, there's something we've turned up, think you ought to look into."

Bob Pettit absorbed the message unenthusiastically, but while he was an inexperienced young policeman, he was a smart one, capable of learning from his prior encounter with violent crime. This time he restrained whatever minimal impulse he might have had to go over to the Stoddard place. Instead, he applied the rule of government workers the world over to kick the ball away before it stops rolling and you end up stuck with it yourself: He contacted the state police. "Hi," he said, "this is Pettit over at the Appleboro station. Think we got a problem you guys will want to look into. Yeah."

Half an hour later, a police car rolled up in front of Ben Stoddard's home. They found him in the little dining room he had converted into an office with a desk and bookshelves. He had been shot, probably with a .22. He lay there quiet as he had never been in life. It might have been wondered whether he had taken any consolation before he died in knowing that he was meeting up with the juiciest piece of gossip of his whole shabby existence, the story of his own demise.

There was indeed something of an odor, though not as much as the overheated postman had claimed.

When Dolly heard the news, she threw up, as predicted, but fortunately she was home at the time, and the U.S. mails escaped unsullied. (As a point of information, she targeted the rag rug next to the phone.) And the next morning, when Hugh Morrison heard the news on arriving at the station house, he sighed deeply. He knew he had frightened the little man by that bit of fiction about his big mouth putting him in danger. Apparently his words weren't as totally fictional as he himself had thought. As the poet said, nature imitates art.

CHAPTER 27

May 15: Lady Slipper

"I DON'T KNOW why," Harriet said, "you insist on taking me out to dinner when I can do something at home that's better to eat, better for you, and Lord knows how much cheaper. And it beats me why we have to cross the mountain, galloping all the way up here to the Catskills to find a restaurant."

"Well for one thing," Morrison explained, "getting away from Appleboro saves your reputation." He snorted.

"What are you laughing at? Think nobody'd believe I could lose my reputation? Don't provoke me, Hugh Morrison. Besides, what am I supposed to save it for, my next incarnation? I'm serious, so don't put me off with these flip remarks."

"Okay, you want a straight answer?" He pointed at his plate, waving a finger over a baked potato struggling for visibility from under a mound of sour cream and chives, an unsavory mess of green beans drowning in butter and dill, and a bloody steak. "Sometimes I need this kind of thing, Harriet, and you won't let me have it. Besides, you can't keep spending money on me. Not right, it isn't."

"That's a sexist attitude," Harriet said scornfully. "And you think I spend too much money, we can split the

159

bill. This is the way you were when we first met. Well, I'm one little woman who doesn't have to have the big strong man take care of her. What I ought to do is turn you over to Judith Oostdyk, let a dainty, timid, ladylike creature turn you into mincemeat."

Morrison deliberately put an enormous gob of potato and sour cream in his mouth and spoke through it, mushily. "Might be fun. I always like a filly with spirit." He ducked as a crumb of bread flew his way. Then it came to him that perhaps in another context he had been something of a sexist to have left Judith Oostdyk out of his calculations. "Say, old girl, do you think your buddy Judith is capable of murder?"

"Now that you ask, in a word—no. That's a frivolous question. And I wonder if it isn't some nasty underlying attitude that gets you thinking a woman who doesn't sit home popping blueberry muffins into an oven must be some kind of degenerate freak, a murderer. If that's the way you look at it, don't turn your back on me, I warn you."

"Wouldn't dream of it. How about some coconut-cream pie, kid? I hear the cholesterol in this place is superb, really first class. No, I mean it, Harriet. This is a serious question. If you had to vote for murderer, whom would you pick first, Judith Oostdyk or Henry?"

Reluctantly, Harriet allowed herself to appear mollified. "That depends. Murderer of who? I mean whom?"

"Yeah," Morrison observed ruefully, "there's a choice, isn't there? Well, let's say Ben Stoddard's murder." Harriet's face was troubled and he hastened to add, "Honestly, Harriet, I'm not being frivolous, believe me. I know I don't tell you everything, and you know I can't, but bear with me, okay?"

"I believe you. Really, I do. And with the understanding that I don't see either of my friends as potential killers, I'll answer. Henry Oostdyk would never under any circumstances be capable of hurting anybody, not merely

160

because he's too kind or decent or civilized but because he can't make a decision to save his soul. And that'd go double for violent action. Look at it this way: Henry is Hamlet in a three-piece suit with a pocket watch. He natters everything to pieces until the problem dies of old age, not murder, or until it's too late anyway. That's why his bank is in trouble, the way I understand it. The poor man is constipated in the head."

"And his wife?"

"You're not going to get me to say Judith could commit murder. All I'll tell you is that she's less incapable of it than her husband. She hates to be frustrated by anybody or anything and she takes steps to make sure she's not. And she'll always find the other party wrong, no matter what."

"For example?"

Harriet pursed her lips and thought hard. "Listen, Hugh, you're still a cop, so I'm going to have to give you the most innocent kind of example I can think of." Morrison nodded his acquiescence. "As you probably can guess, Judith is a culture vulture. She collects cultural shreds and tucks them into her head as if they were china figurines on her shelves. I'd bet when she goes to Europe, which they used to do regularly, she's so busy putting check marks on a list headed 'Cathedrals I Have Seen' that she never gets to look at the fool things properly. More specifically, last winter she dragooned a number of us into going over to her place Sunday afternoons to listen to the Philharmonic broadcasts. She's got this magnificent stereo system, and a few of us agreed.

"Anyway, Judy chattered away without stopping to breathe, couldn't have caught a note, but after it was over, she shushed us all so she could listen to the announcer tell us what we had heard. Or not heard, as was certainly the case. Unfortunately, Ella McCollum kept talking and Judith never found out what piece it was she should have been adding to her collection. Later, she said to me that

161

that was the last time Ella was going to be asked to one of the broadcast afternoons. 'Babble, babble, that's all the woman knows to do,' she told me. I suppose what I'm saying is that Judy can't bear being frustrated, even in the smallest detail, and that she can always find someone else to blame and to punish. But murder, no. And that's all I'm going to say on the subject."

Morrison thought that he himself might be able to say something more on the subject, that a lady contemplating the murder of Ben Stoddard because he talked too much about a certain inexpensive gemstone would scarcely call attention to herself beforehand by wagging the gemstone over to drop into a policeman's outstretched hand. Then again, it was frequently the case that inhibited types such as husband Henry would burst forth under accumulated pressure and take uncharacteristic action, sometimes of the most violent variety. And yet again, maybe he was looking in the wrong direction altogether. On the one hand, this; on the other hand, that; and on the third hand, something else again. Less thought and more action was what he needed right now, and as a matter of fact, he had the germ of an idea, a plan beginning to take on a hazy outline in his mind. It might inspire somebody to take steps whom he hadn't considered, but he'd need help to get it started, and not from another cop. Maybe Harriet? First he had to know how far she'd be willing to go; whether she'd balk at playing tricks on a friend who might just be a killer.

"Listen, Harriet," he said, "you keep saying you're not about to sit around and wait for me or anybody else to find out what happened to Jason Belding; that you're going to do whatever you can to bring things to a head. That right?"

Harriet looked at him suspiciously. She nodded.

"Okay. Does that go for Ben Stoddard's death, too?"

"What are you getting at?"

"I'll tell you some other time. For now, just give me an answer."

162

"All right, yes, if there was anything I could do, I'd do it. Not just for Jason, but for Ben, too. And as far as that goes, for anybody else. As long as I'm alive."

"You sound pretty strong about that, don't you?"

"Damn right I do."

"Why?"

Harriet looked startled. "Why? I don't know exactly how to put it, but let's say it's just to prove that I'm still here, that I'm still breathing, still able to do something."

"Tell me more."

"Hugh, have you ever taken a long plane trip, where you had to sit still for five or six hours of tedium?" Morrison nodded. "Then maybe you know the feeling you can get that the flight attendants are going down the other aisle with trays full of exotic gourmet delights, practically forcing them on the passengers with great gales of merry laughter. And nobody comes down your aisle. And then at mealtime, they always seem to get to you half an hour after everybody else and they're out of whatever your choice might have been. Then they pass you over when they're serving the wine or coffee because they're so busy chatting it up with people their own age that they simply don't see you when they go by.

"You begin to think you're invisible, and that invisibility sets in with age. I didn't feel it so strongly when Jason was still around, but now I'm afraid it may be getting worse. Well, I'm not going to let them make me invisible. I don't mind being irrelevant to young people, because they're irrelevant to me, too. If they don't want to listen to the music I like because it's old-fashioned, that's fine, because what they like is just a lot of noise to me and I won't sit still for it. Fair enough, as far as it goes. But damn it, I'm still here! I can still be seen; I can still jump up and down, break windows, throw cream pies, and dance a fandango, and I'm not going to let myself be convinced otherwise.

"Do you understand what I mean, Hugh? I'm part

163

of this world until I leave it, and in my own dotty and probably incompetent way, I'll do what I have to do even if there are a lot of people who can't see me when I walk past. End of sermon."

"Good for you. And I'm convinced. If I had an honorary sheriff's badge, I'd pin it on you, and I'm going to take up that offer of help. I warn you that I'm asking you to trick somebody, a friend of yours. If I'm right, your friend is a murderer. If I'm wrong, you'll have made a damn fool of yourself." He grinned. "And whichever way it goes, you may wish you'd had a little of that invisibility you've been griping about."

"Try me."

He did. "Okay, here's what I want you to do. Now don't ask me why, because I can't tell you yet." He explained what he wanted.

"Oh, Hugh, that's just plain sneaky! Nasty! I couldn't!"

"Suit yourself." He waved a hand at the waitress to get the check.

"I'll do it. They may run me out of town for it, but I'll do it."

"Atta girl. Gotta work out the details first. Tell you soon. Let's go."

164

CHAPTER 28

May 17: Showy Orchis

"**J**UDY, DEAR," HENRY Oostdyk said, "what would you say if we let that New York City crew have the bank. They'd give me a two-, three-year contract to stay on, and we could work out the payments over a number of years, keep the taxes low. What do you think?"

Whatever Judith was thinking, she didn't say. Her expression said a lot, though, and it was largely negative.

"And after about six months, I'm sure they'd be only too delighted, if we wanted it, to buy up my contract. We could move up to Kingston, if we wanted, get a nice little place, maybe even one of the old stone houses, and take things easy."

"Leave Appleboro? Leave our home here?" She sounded as if she had been invited to leave Planet Earth for residence on a space station. "That'd be awful, Henry. We couldn't! Anyway, *I* couldn't! How can you even think of such a thing!"

"It isn't that I want to think of it, but we've got to be practical. I thought that with Jason Belding dead—I hate to sound vicious, but I thought that all our troubles would be over. But now with Harriet Lorimer acting up—" He spread his hands helplessly. "And while the bank is still in reasonably good shape, we'd do a lot better to sell out now than if we wait till things get worse."

"But they won't get worse. They can't!"

Henry smiled sadly. "I'm afraid they will. Let's face it."

"I could kill that woman! She's so unreasonable! I tried to talk to her the other day, but she won't listen. She and Jason Belding were a pair, all right. Let's not even talk about it for a while. Let's just think about things, all right? You fix drinks while I go see about dinner. And get the smoked nuts out of the cupboard."

They both thought about things quietly. Their thoughts must have traveled down the same road, for when they sat down over cocktails, Judith was trying to phrase an innocent question about the contents of the downstairs medicine cabinet when Henry suddenly said, "Not to change the subject, Judy—or maybe I should say to change the subject, what in heaven's name got into you the other day to throw away all the junk that's been piling up in the bathroom chest? I mean, after years and years, you suddenly up and start clearing out."

"Oh, it got so messy in there. Every time you open the door, a tube or a bottle of God knows what would come falling out. So I just chucked it, that's all. Why do you ask? Did I toss out anything you still wanted?" Her voice sounded terribly casual.

"No, no, no. Just asking. Just curious, I suppose." His voice was just as casual.

Neither casual tone was very convincing; gemstones and pills hardly ever mix well, and even less often do they make for casual conversation at cocktails or any other time.

When Elfrida Von Hesse's back ached, she always threw a cushion onto the Windsor rocker and sat straight back to rest her weary frame. This afternoon, however, despite her backache, she sat slumped in the rocker and got no relief whatsoever. But the peculiar thing was that she failed to notice it, so preoccupied was she with her thoughts.

There's hate and crime and evil in the town, she mused. Jason Belding dead, Ben Stoddard dead. How did it happen? Who started all this? Could Henry Oostdyk have ever been capable of—? No. Judith? She didn't answer herself but tucked her hands under her arms for warmth. (The temperature was almost 70 degrees.) She rocked in the chair, only half-conscious of what she was doing. On the tilt forward, she asked, Who?; and on the backward motion, she murmured, Why? Who? Why? Who? Why?

No one answered, but the water boiling on the stove for tea evaporated and scorched the pot.

Carl Van Houten was slumped at his desk, too, in his New York office. He didn't mind playing in the mud, he told himself, but when you're in deep shit, there's no point in trying to swim across. Just get the hell out and cut your losses. The Lorimer woman wasn't going to play ball on the Belding right-of-way, and the old bastard Jessup had died without a will, so his property would be tied up in court for years. Every crook of a politician in the county and in Albany would be selling off the land for legal fees over the next five years until there wasn't enough left to build an outhouse on. So the hell with Appleboro. No matter which way he turned, the lawyers would be chewing on his flesh, the stinking vultures. You try to do something for the old hometown and what do they do, they dump on you. Well, screw 'em all. Let the place rot; he was pulling out. He'd salvage whatever lumber he could, whatever that old nut hadn't managed to burn, and he'd burn it himself before he'd let anybody in that asshole place get their mitts on it for free.

And that miserable creep Chris Morton walking out on him for a job in Florida. No gratitude. He buzzed for Doris. As she walked in, he bent over the office checkbook.

"Yes, Mr. Van Houten?"

"Doris, here's a check for two weeks' salary. I want you out of here by lunch. Lotsa luck." He looked at her hard, daring her to react.

The woman took the check. "I know you've been

interviewing other girls, Mr. Van Houten, so don't look at me like you expected me to break down and cry. Frankly, I'm relieved."

"Just pack your chewing gum and go, will you? Can the chitchat. The new girl comes in at one, and I want you out before then."

"That's a good idea, sir. I'll pack my chewing gum and go. Anybody else, I'd park it between his eyes, but with you, there isn't enough room between your eyes." She spun about and marched out. There was a crash from the outer office and Doris's voice carried in. "Oh, Mr. Van Houten, you know that Leerdam vase of yours? Well, it just got broke. 'Bye now." The outer door slammed.

Georgia Belding bent over and picked up a pair of socks one of the kids had peeled off the night before and let lie where it fell. "I wish those kids would learn," she muttered.

Billy was reading the paper over his morning coffee and in an abstracted voice said, "They will. Just give 'em time."

"I'll give 'em time, Billy, but meanwhile you could give me a hand."

"Huh?"

"You heard. I thought when Dad went and the property was sold, I'd be able to have a woman in three or four times a week, but that's not going to be, is it?"

"Afraid not. You'll have to go on suffering with a once-a-week maid, poor thing. God knows, I tried to work something out, but that's the way it goes. All that planning, all that work, and for nothing."

"What planning? What work? What did you do, and all for nothing, the way you put it?"

"What do you mean, what'd I do? What's that supposed to mean?" Billy's voice rose.

"Hey, just one damned minute, you. It's getting so I can't say anything without you flying off the handle. I ask a simple question and you act like I'm accusing you of, of—

168

Billy, is there something I ought to know? Anything you want to tell me. What the hell's bugging you these days?"

Billy slapped down his coffee cup. "Jesus H. Christ!" he snapped. "I've got to get to the office, keep you in theater tickets, orchestra seats. My wife, the helpmeet. Hah!" He finished dressing without another word and left, not quite slamming the front door, but not shutting it very gently, either.

"What'd I do?" Georgia asked herself. "All I did was ask—" She put a hand over her mouth as if to stop the thought before it took conscious form in her mind.

Harriet picked up the phone and followed Hugh Morrison's instructions.

"Hello? How are you today? I'm in a terrible state myself. All these awful things going on. Yes, me, too. Makes a body almost sorry to be living here. Yes, and it's been such a wonderful place to live, all of us good friends and everything. No, I don't think it'll ever be the same again because I've just heard something, and it's so dreadful I don't know which way to turn, honestly.

"I don't think I ought to say anything. Really. It'll only upset you the way it's upset me, and if it should turn out to be a false alarm, well, I hate gossip. I mean, God knows Ben was a good friend, and I shouldn't speak ill of the dead, but that was the one thing I could never stand about him. I know you did. We all felt that way.

"Well, the thing is, you know I've become sort of friendly with that state trooper. Hugh Morrison. No, nothing like that, silly! It's only that, well, since it was Jason, I've been pestering him to keep me informed of any developments, and I suppose I've even been a little brazen about it, but I don't care. I couldn't just sit about and wait quietly, now could I?

"But that's not what I'm worried about now. It's something else and I feel awful about it and I had to talk to someone. The thing is, Morrison has been a little careless about what he's been saying to me, and I just know from what he's let slip that he expects to be taking Henry Oostdyk in and charging him! Isn't that too awful! No, no, you don't understand! It's not about Jason; the darned fool is going to charge Henry with Ben Stoddard's death.

"Of course it's ridiculous! I know that well as you. If anybody in that household could commit murder, it'd be Judith, and she couldn't do it, either. But a sweet, gentle man like Henry. You know, I think this could kill him, if it happens. No, I don't think it'll be right away. I gather he's not ready yet. I don't know, a couple of days, maybe.

"What? Oh. Well, call me back when you get a chance. I need to talk to someone, I'm that upset. I'll be home tonight, watching TV; there's this 'Masterpiece Theatre' rerun on PBS I missed the first time. Now don't you go fretting too much like me. We'll have to wait and see. And pray."

When Harriet hung up, she expelled her breath furiously, as if she had been holding back a scream. Her throat was tight and dry, and she trotted into the kitchen to inspect the contents of the refrigerator. She rejected the ice water, needing more of a lift than that could provide. She studied the diet cola but rejected it as well in favor of a soft drink loaded with tooth-rotting sugar and waist-destroying calories. There are times, she told herself, when a body is entitled, plain entitled.

Dutifully, she headed back to call Hugh, who would be waiting at the phone in his office.

"Morrison," he grunted.

"It's me. Harriet."

"Hi. How'd it go?"

"It was awful. Practically hung up on me. I said to call me back tonight, that I'd be watching TV, but Hugh, I'm not going to sit home and wait. I'm not. In fact, this time you can take me out to dinner. You owe me and I'm going to spend a week's salary for you."

"Sure. Let's go classy. How about the Old Dutch Tavern?"

170

"No. Their idea of gourmet cuisine is to put pine nuts in everything, including the chicken soup, and double the prices."

"Mountain Top Inn? The dining room isn't reserved for only the hotel guests anymore."

"Oh, they get such an elderly crowd, all those people getting over heart attacks, it'd just depress me. Besides, anybody under ninety walks in the hotel door, I think you have to have a note from your mother before they'll let you stay."

"Okay, then, what do you want? You name it."

"I don't know. I can't think. Maybe I'm not hungry. Maybe I ought to just stay home and watch that TV rerun. Suppose we should go out and the phone starts to ring while we're gone, and suppose that—"

"Whoa! You calm yourself down, Harriet, and stop the maybes and the supposes. I'll be over later and meanwhile you can think about where you want to go, and if you want your precious TV, you can set up that VCR thing you've got and record it, okay? Now take a deep breath and relax, you hear?"

"I'll try, Hugh, and I'll set up the VCR. I'm okay now, I promise. But maybe— Oh, my God, I just realized something! Oh, Hugh, I'm such a fool!" Harriet's voice went up; in another context someone might have concluded a sheep was bleating.

"Now what is it? Take it easy, girl. What's the trouble?"

With difficulty, she pulled her voice down an octave and said quietly, though with a certain tremor, "Hugh, I've been blind. And stupid, and I've misled you. Jason wasn't killed on December 5. It happened the day before. It happened December 4, during the day, before he could put Jezebel out for the night. I know it. I'm positive!"

CHAPTER 29

May 17–18: Blue Flag

*T*HEY WOUND UP in the local vegetarian restaurant, at Hugh's suggestion. "How come this place?" Harriet asked. "I hardly ever think of you and tofu burgers as a couple. You going native, Morrison? Been hanging around with me and the brown-rice set too long?"

"Not a chance. You were in such a swivet, I figured you'd be at my throat if we went somewhere I could get a decent slab of beef. Believe me, if I had known you were going to cool down this fast, I would've picked a chophouse."

"Well, I'm glad you didn't. And now that I've had a chance to think about it, I'm sort of pleased with myself. Not about that phone call, but because I finally figured out that Jason had to have been killed on the fourth. It was really so obvious, I'm almost ashamed of myself for not seeing it before."

"All because of the VCR, huh?"

Harriet nodded. "All because of the VCR. I've told you how methodical Jason was, that he would have rewound that tape first thing the morning of the fifth if he'd been able to." Her voice trembled slightly. "But when you took me up there, you saw that I had to rewind it myself. I set the thing to record the night of the fourth, that Dietrich film he wanted. Jason was always after me for not rewinding soon as possible. He said it stretched the tape to leave it in the middle. That's why he had the box out on the coffee table, so's he'd see it first thing in the morning and get right down to rewinding."

"Yeah, but the calendar was open to the fifth. You said he was methodical about that, too. How come he would have turned to the fifth a day in advance? You can't have it both ways."

"Don't you see, Hugh? He made notes to himself about what he had to do the day he left—take the cat away, unplug the TV set, turn off the pump. And he had it open to the fifth because he knew he'd be thinking of new things to take care of before he left. He always said he had a mind like a sieve and that he had to write things down or he'd probably even forget he was leaving."

"Well, maybe. It's a possibility, anyway. Worth a try, I guess, seeing how we're not getting anywhere as it is."

"Try not to be so enthusiastic, Officer. It's bad for the blood pressure. I know I'm right. I think that's why I've calmed down; I've finally done something, finally figured something out."

"Believe me, I'm not criticizing. In fact, I'm grateful. We need a new angle. And as far as the old blood pressure goes, one more taste of Our Special Soy Bean Wiggle"—he pointed at the menu—"and it'll be down below zero. But I'm a fool for duty." He lifted a forkful to his mouth. "Actually, it isn't too bad. Especially if lumpy farina is your bag."

When Hugh took Harriet home, they could hear her phone ringing from out front. Harriet took the standard female forever to dig her keys out from under Eocene layers of tissues, Pleistocene tiers of eyeglasses, and Paleolithic strata of assorted gloves, lists, memorabilia of places and events whose provenance was long lost in his-

173

tory, plus artifacts clearly present on a social call from another galaxy. Excavatory haste made waste.

"I'll get it," Morrison blurted, and as Harriet continued her search for whichever came first, her keys or the Holy Grail, he slipped a plastic credit card along the edge of the door and eased back the latch.

"Don't you dare," Harriet said, appreciably after the fact.

But the policeman was already down the hall and lifting the phone. "Hello?"

"Oh. Is this 255–72— Is Mrs. Lorimer there?"

"Who's calling, please?"

By way of answer, the caller broke the connection.

Harriet entered, still jamming the archeological detritus back into storage. "Hugh, I wish you wouldn't do that! This is still my house, and I resent your breaking in and taking over!"

"But Harriet, I was pretty sure it was the call we were expecting. And it was."

"Yes, and I see they hung up on you, didn't they? Serves you right. Next time, please do me the courtesy of letting me open my own door. And answering my own phone. That is, if you don't mind."

Harriet, Morrison reasoned, was feeling a renewed surge of guilt at having cooperated with the police, and it was his assignment, all but spelled out in detail in the rules of behavior for the minions of the law, to stand still under the lash and offer a wholesome mash of remorse, gratitude, and humility in return. For no one but Harriet would he have played his assigned part in the charade. "I'm sorry, Harriet. I was almost certain it was that call and I didn't want to miss it."

"And you missed it anyway, didn't you?" Harriet snapped. "They hung up. I do wish you wouldn't try to take over, Hugh. I got into this against my better judgment, and now you've got the idea you can do whatever you please. Well I'm sorry, but that's not the way it's going to be. You just listen to me, Hugh Morrison, and pay attention to what I'm going to tell you," she said, wagging a finger. But after she opened her mouth, nothing came out, so she subsided. "Oh, hell, what difference does it make," she said softly. "I'm on edge. Sorry. But they did hang up, didn't they?"

"That's right. Soon as they recognized my voice."

"What happens next?"

"We wait. Or I wait. If you were called back once, there'll be another call later, maybe even one to me. In fact, most likely to me. They're on the simmer, and a good simmer comes to a boil, long as they think the heat's still on high. Good people make lousy criminals."

"And this is good people," Harriet said sadly.

"That's right."

"It isn't fair," she added. "It isn't fair."

"That's right, too. But neither is violent death."

CHAPTER 30

May 21: Grape Hyacinth

THREE AND A half days later and nothing had happened. Morrison began to feel like a fool for pontificating to Harriet about the criminal mind and the urge to confess, especially the better class of criminal mind. He might have considered keeping his mouth shut, he told himself, maybe saying only that it was likely they'd call back again. For two days Harriet had continued to ask whether anything had developed; then she had knocked it off, probably out of embarrassment.

Time to cut out the maundering. Time to encourage a little action from that upper crust of Appleboro criminals he had been so pompous about. Everybody loves a big brass band. He'd give them better, right down the middle of Main Street, and see who, if anybody, would be inspired to get into the parade. If anybody . . .

A white police car, Senior Investigator Morrison at the wheel, with Senior Investigator Morrison allowing full voice to the siren, staged a stately progress down Main Street. Shopkeepers and their customers ran to look and were puzzled by a blasting siren when the driver wasn't trying to make time or to move traffic to one side. Teenagers with ghetto blasters on their shoulders, their ears pressed tightly to the speakers, were annoyed to find themselves dealing with decibel ratings more offensive than those they could produce themselves. A few spaced-out youngsters, either students or the hangers-on that breed in the streets around schools like algae in a stagnant pond, sprawling on the sidewalk near their favorite eatery, lifted one or both eyebrows (depending on how much strength remained to them for violent exertion after the ingestion of whatever had been decreed the controlled substance of choice by the arbiters of the day).

It was thus a near certainty that every soul in downtown Appleboro witnessed the police car draw up majestically in front of the Georgian-style bank (red brick, white woodwork, center door with two large windows to each side, nonfunctioning clock in tower), where a police officer emerged and strutted through the double doors with the arrogance of the corrupt sheriff in a movie about the Old West.

And I hope they all got a good look, Morrison said to himself.

They did, and news of the trooper's march into the bank, past the receptionist and, via a secretary, into Henry Oostdyk's office was reported from the movie house to the diner, the hardware store to the library, the supermarket to the real estate office.

Henry Oostdyk looked up as Morrison was ushered in, his expression midway between perplexity and anxiety. The policeman answered the unasked question. "Sorry about the siren," he lied. "I went over a pothole just this side of the bridge and the fool thing came on and stayed that way until I turned off the ignition. Have to take a look under the hood before I get going again." He smiled reassuringly.

"Quite a ruckus. From what I can see out the window, the town's lined up waiting for you to take the James boys out in chains. Frankly, I'm relieved myself that's all it is. Now, what can I do for you, sir?"

"Just checking on a few details and I wondered if you've got your time clock records handy for a few days before last December fifth. Of course you know we've been going ahead on the theory that Mr. Belding was murdered on the fifth, but we're looking into some other possibilities now and I want to check everyone out again. No problems on our part and I hope none on yours, sir."

"No, no, I understand. I can't say it's a pleasure, but I'm glad to help. Let me get my secretary on it." He flipped open the intercom on the desk and spoke the appropriate words. Two minutes later, a selection of time cards was on his desk. "Here we are now," he said. "Let's see. I've got the second, third, and fourth of December right here. That enough for you?"

Morrison nodded. "Plenty." He held out a hand.

Oostdyk looked quickly before he passed the information over. "I can't be lucky every time, I suppose. I punched out for long lunch hours on the second and third, it looks like." He laughed. "Don't tell the board of governors on me, okay? And on the fourth, I was gone a good part of the afternoon."

Morrison looked at the cards. "Any notion about where you might have been that afternoon?"

The banker looked mildly reproachful. "Hey, it's May now. I can't even begin to guess. Could've been the dentist—I could check that—or shopping, or I could have plain goofed off and gone home. Even bankers are sometimes human, though lots of folks would be happy to deny it." He laughed; Morrison smiled.

"Can't hang you for that, sir. I'll have to take these along for now, let you have them back as soon as possible. There's one other thing. I've got something down in the station I need you to look at. I'm sorry I can't take it out and bring it here, but that's the way it is with crucial evidence. You understand," he said confidentially, hoping

Oostdyk wouldn't question him. "If you can spare the time, I can run you down and have you back again in half an hour."

"Can you tell me what's it about?"

"I'd rather not. It'd be simpler all around if you could take a couple of minutes off and come with me. I'd sure appreciate it."

Oostdyk's face said he wasn't entirely sure he liked the idea, but he said, quite slowly, "Well, I'm rather busy at the moment, but—half an hour, you say?" Morrison nodded. "Okay, let's get on with it. Though it does seem odd."

It sure ought to seem odd, Morrison agreed silently. The two men stood and left after Oostdyk spoke a few words to his secretary. They got in the police car together, with Morrison remembering at the last moment to get out again and fiddle about under the hood. "Siren's disconnected now," he said as he took the driver's seat again. He wondered, as he put the key in the ignition, whether the siren would go off for real this time as a punishment for his fibbing, the way his mother might have predicted it would.

There were still sufficient busybodies abroad waiting to see what real-life adventure was transpiring in Appleboro so that the word was bound to spread again: The banker man was being driven off in the police car. Soon they knew all about it in front of the movie house, inside the diner, in the aisles of the hardware store, alongside the stacks in the library, next to the gourmet deli counter in the supermarket, and at the desks in the real estate office. Every last soul in Appleboro knew that Henry Oostdyk was being taken to the police station, with the sole exception of Mrs. Mintz, who had misplaced her hearing aid and was therefore unaware of the persistent ringing of her telephone; beside, she was suffering from an acute overload of medicinal brandy.

179

CHAPTER 31

May 21: Ragged Robin

HE KNEW, MORE or less, *what* Oostdyk
was going to say, but he did have a certain gloomy curiosity
as to exactly *how* the man would put it. Exactly how the
man would lie. "Now then, sir, this is what I want you to
look at." He opened the box on the desk between them.
"I'd like you to identify this, if you can. Have you ever
seen it before?"

Oostdyk bent over the key chain, frowned, and
said, "May I pick it up?" Morrison nodded. He also wished
the man would play out the game without spending the day
on it; maybe he could doze off for a few minutes while
waiting. "Take your time," he said, not meaning a word of
it. It was all so tedious.

"No, I don't . . . really . . . think so." He looked
up at the policeman, and seeing an expression of weary disbelief, he withdrew to a safer position. "Oh, wait a minute.
Why, I do believe— Why, of course! It's Jason Belding's!
But I don't understand. Why ask me? I mean, out of all the
people in Appleboro . . . I don't understand," he repeated.

His expression was an appeal for help, so Morrison,
coplike, remained silent, blinking once or twice like a frog

patiently waiting on a log for a swimmer to stop roiling the waters and finish drowning.

"And you've even taken me away from the bank in the middle of the day. Mr. Morrison, I simply don't understand what this is all about, and if that's all, I'd like to get back." He shook his head in annoyance. (The swimmer, making a valiant effort to stay afloat.)

"Yeah," Morrison said, which could have meant anything. "Couple uh questions." (Why, he wondered, did he so often fall into a tough cop accent at times like this? Too many movies?) "Tell me, Mr. Oostdyk, what was the last time you saw this?"

"How can I possibly remember that? It's only a key chain. I suppose the last time I saw Jason take his keys out, whenever that might have been. I don't understand—" Oostdyk had the uneasy feeling that he had said he didn't understand something more times than absolutely necessary. "I don't see how any of this is going to help you."

Again, Morrison ignored the timid outburst. "Funny. The way I get it is that you had this gizmo in your possession for a while. In your home, the way I get it."

"That's ridiculous. How would I come to have Jason Belding's key chain?" He saw, or thought he saw, the mildly cynical reproach on his interrogator's face. "Who could have said such a thing?"

"Mr. Stoddard," Morrison said very quickly, very quietly. "Mr. Benjamin Stoddard, before he died. He told me personally. And so we can save a little time and you can get back to your office, I can add to that that he saw it in a medicine cabinet in your home. And," he concluded with a slight embellishment on the truth, "I have a signed deposition from him to that effect."

Henry Oostdyk held up both his hands to the level of his chest and patted the air, as if he were trying to soothe an overexcited child. "All right. I've been foolish. Yes, I had it in my medicine cabinet, tucked into an old bottle of pills. I found the fool thing, months ago, long before Jason was killed, and I simply didn't recognize it. I mean, what the devil, it's the kind of thing a woman is more likely to pay attention to." His face brightened. "I took it to Jenke's Jewelry, right there in the plaza near the bank, and asked him what it was. You can check that out with him yourself. Jenke's!" He sat back and sighed with relief.

"Anyway, Fred Jenke told me it didn't amount to much, so I figured it wasn't worth it to put an ad in the lost and found column. It was such a pretty little thing, that star in it and all, that I was going to have it made up into something for my wife for our anniversary. Then I started to wonder; that seemed like such a cheap thing to do, like cheating Judith." He stopped and stared at the floor, pondering the moral and other consequences of cheating Judith with a found gemstone of no special value.

"Where'd you find it?"

"In a field. Walking up to my property over Jason's land. It was right in the middle of the path."

Morrison wondered bitterly if all the Oostdyks, the kids, too, had this talent for finding jewels in the countryside around Appleboro. Maybe they could go into business, open a mine, find diamonds while they were at it. "Why'd you keep it in a medicine cabinet?"

"Because Judith would have found it just about anyplace else in the house. She neatens all the time. Every bureau drawer, every closet. You know how it is with women." He smiled at Morrison, unsuccessfully trying to establish a fond conspiracy of boys contemplating the lovable foibles of the womenfolk, bless 'em. "And even that didn't work, because she cleaned out the old medicines and chucked everything out." He looked startled. "But how did you get hold of it, Mr. Morrison?"

Morrison ignored the question. "Then you're telling me you had no idea who the owner was when you found it?"

"Well . . . not at first. After Jason was killed we

182

talked about him all the time, about him and his wife and the years here in Appleboro. Then I remembered one day. And I'm ashamed to say I was too frightened to come forward and say anything."

"Why?"

"I think you know. In your position, I would have looked at me as a very likely suspect. I stood to profit, or thought I did, from Jason's death. And to say I had the man's key chain, well, I mean—"

"Then why didn't you throw it out?"

"I meant to. I wanted to. Then I'd start to think that that would have been wrong. I knew I should have come forward with it, and I thought it'd be smarter to keep my mouth shut and chuck the thing, and—well, there you are; I couldn't bring myself to do anything at all." He lowered his head and looked at the floor until, possibly out of some hazy notion that the town banker should project an image of confidence and strength, he said, "But see here, Mr. Morrison, I can't see what possible significance any of this can have. This is a total waste of time, my time and yours." The words were firm, but the music, the tone of his voice, was as unconvincing as "The Star-Spangled Banner" played on a kazoo. Just the way Harriet had described him. Hamlet in a three-piece suit.

A trooper knocked and came into the room. "'Scuse me, sir, you got someone waiting to see you. Says it's urgent."

Morrison nodded. "Where've you got them?" The trooper told him. "Good. I want you to make sure the door of that room is closed. Then come back here and you can drive Mr. Oostdyk to his office. Okay?"

"Yes, sir."

Morrison stood. "I think that covers everything for now, Mr. Oostdyk. The trooper'll drive you back. I'll only say that you could have saved yourself and the police a lot of time and trouble if you had told us your story from the beginning instead of making us come and get it."

183

"I'm sorry. I should have."

Morrison ignored whatever apology there was in the man's words and watched the officer escort Oostdyk into the patrol car. His story was ridiculous, but given his character, it had the ring of truth. It was much more likely that he, rather than his wife, had found the key chain in a field somewhere. Once again he wished the Oostdyks would get together and try to get a little variety in their stories. At any rate, the chances were that the police still weren't finished with this couple, except for the moment. Right now Morrison's guess was that Henry's story was more or less true and that the wife had found the key ring in the medicine chest. By then Stoddard, of course, had been shooting his mouth off all over town. She'd have realized she couldn't simply throw the damned thing out, so she decided to bluff it through by turning it in before the police came for it. All to protect her Henry.

Now he had to see the visitor. He knew who it was, who it had to be. He hoped he was wrong, but he was certain he was right. Almost certain. Why do nice people, innocent people, for God's sake!, have to turn out to be guilty? With that unanswerable question in his mind, he went out the door and down the hall. What a lousy job!

He opened the door that he had ordered shut to conceal Henry Oostdyk's departure, and nodded at the figure seated stiffly on a chair. It was an uncomfortable room in which to wait, perhaps deliberately so. The walls were institutional buff, scuffed over the years by police and by cleanup personnel whose feelings about the place were somewhere in between unconcern and resentment. The long cheap table was scarred by cigarette burns, and in the days when such few women as were on the force wore skirts instead of the current trousers, there had been bitter complaints about stockings snagged on the splintered legs. The chairs matched, except for the one now occupied, which was covered in a cheap leather substitute, periodically torn (or slashed) and scarcely deserving the sobriquet

184

of easy chair except as a term of derision. The room did not so much advise that hope be abandoned by all entering its confines as it suggested that anyone entering had to be nuts to begin with if they did so voluntarily.

Morrison nodded. "Good morning. What can I do for you?" He sat on one of the wooden chairs, first placing a doubled piece of cardboard under the left rear leg, which was shorter than the other three. They kept the cardboard on the window ledge for that purpose. There was never any danger that the cleaning crew would throw it out.

"Henry Oostdyk is here? You brought him in?"

"I brought him in, yes," Morrison said, not answering both parts of the query but not precisely lying.

With clenched fists, the visitor said, "You've got to let him go. He didn't do it. I know he didn't."

"Didn't do what, ma'am?"

She looked at him scornfully. "Don't play cat and mouse with me, sir. You know perfectly well what I mean. Henry Oostdyk didn't kill Ben Stoddard."

"Did anyone say he did, Miss Von Hesse? Tell me about it."

"I know what you're up to," Elfie said in a quiet fury, "and you're wrong. You've got to let him go. He's incapable of taking life. I know that. I know he didn't do it. I know it!"

"I'm afraid, ma'am, you'll have to do better than that. How could you possibly know such a thing?"

"Because—because I killed Ben Stoddard. I'm sorry I did it, but he was a vicious, sneaky man, out to hurt people, and for no other reason than his own amusement." She stared straight at the policeman. Her eyes were over-bright and they were red. Henry Oostdyk's eyes were over-bright, too, Morrison thought, but his were pale and perplexed, while this woman's burned.

"I want you to know, ma'am, that you've got to be careful what you say to me. You realize that whatever you

185

say voluntarily can be used against you. If it should ever come to that."

"I realize that. I've got no choice. You've arrested an innocent man."

Morrison's index finger, right hand, played with the switch under the table that would turn on the recorder. He left it off. "And this may sound strange to you, but," he said with a smile that was almost apologetic, "you'll have to prove what you say. We always say in the department that for every crime, sooner or later you get three confessions," he added in the full knowledge that he had just made up an old adage.

Elfie stared at the man in disbelief. "Why, you think I'm insane, don't you! You think I'm a potty old maid imagining things! Trying to get attention, living out some fantasy or other!"

In a gentle voice, Morrison replied, "No, Miss Von Hesse. It isn't that. I only want you to think hard before you talk, before you get yourself into trouble. Murder is a terrible thing and it has terrible consequences. Let me get us both some coffee, calm things down, and we can talk it over quietly. Okay?" He got up and whispered quietly to a trooper in the room outside.

They both sipped the hot drinks in silence. Morrison's finger toyed with the recorder switch again and finally, endless seconds later, he turned it on. "Now, Miss Von Hesse," he said softly, "now we can talk. Please take your time and be very careful what you say. Please consider every word before you speak, because anything you say may be self-incriminating. And I'd strongly advise you to think about getting yourself a lawyer before you go any further."

"No. I know what I did and I know what I have to do about it. I killed Ben Stoddard. I make no excuses. I killed him." She was calm, too calm, though her clear, even voice cut through the stale air in the room like a surgical knife.

"How did you do it, ma'am? Did you take the knife with you or did you grab one in Mr. Stoddard's house after an argument?"

She looked at Morrison scornfully. "You don't believe me, do you? All you see is another lonely, neurotic woman desperate for attention, screaming that she hates the world as much as it hates her and that she can prove it by killing. Or by saying that she kills. Well, you're a fool, if that's what you think. Listen, you," she said, jabbing a finger at the detective, "you take me seriously, damn you, and don't try to trick me." She sat back and ran a hand over her head, and for the first time in a quarter of a century, that glacial bun of hair was askew, tilted to one side and looking ready to come down. "How can I make you listen!"

"By telling me, Miss Von Hesse. I'll listen. Tell me about it, tell me about the knife."

"Yes, you'll listen, won't you? You'll listen to an old fool screaming, 'I kill, therefore I am,' but you won't believe! That's it, isn't it! That's why you're playing games. Don't patronize me when I speak the truth. You're the fool, not the old crazy woman!" The words were frigid with contempt, hot with fury.

As her voice grew louder and more angry, Morrison's became softer and more gentle. "I don't understand, ma'am. Why would I try to trick you? I need to understand and I want to help. But first, won't you help me? It's not easy to believe a person of your character would kill a man, stab him to death in cold blood."

Elfie banged both her fists on the table. "Stop the charade! Stop it right here!" she snapped. "We both know damned well nobody stabbed Ben Stoddard. I took no knife and I picked up no knife in that creature's house. I shot him, and you know it. Shot him! I took a gun. I took it in case he persisted, he kept on, he . . . he . . ." The rigid discipline and control perfected over so many years was cracking under the strain; the ship that had sailed so tidily

187

through the shoals of deceit was now unpiloted, and the wheel was spinning madly.

"He what?"

Elfie's eyes lost their brightness and her expression grew vague as she reached into her bag and drew out a .22, which she placed on the table between them. Morrison slowly, gently took out a handkerchief and drew the weapon out of the woman's reach. She spoke and the words that came out were propelled more by an inner need than by a desire to communicate, and they floated into space with Morrison not necessarily as their intended target. "My father gave me this when I first came to Appleboro, a hundred years ago. For protection, he said. And he taught me how to use it." She paused briefly. "I didn't want to," she went on in a high, childlike voice, "but he kept saying, he kept laughing about sweaters, about wiping . . . cashmere sweaters, he said, not peasanty, old, scratchy wool ones. . . . His very words." She sobbed. ". . . wipe himself. It was that black star key chain. He was using it like a knife. He was the one with a knife; he was the killer, slashing . . . making decent people look obscene, covering them with dirt, threatening . . . and I couldn't let him. . . . He kept calling me 'dear,' as if the word was a curse. And it was, it was."

She stopped and looked down, staring at nothing. "Wipe himself," she murmured in an echo, and she settled back with a shudder, the fire gone out at last and a deep and empty cold moving in to replace it.

"Miss Von Hesse, that's about enough. You're in no condition to talk. Do you have a lawyer?" There was no response. "Do you know anybody you can call?" Again, silence, punctuated only by the woman's rasping breath, slowly subsiding. "Come with me, then, and we'll see about getting somebody."

Gently, he led her, unresisting, out into the hall. An irrational surge of fury overtook him, and it was directed not at this poor creature but at Henry Oostdyk, a man who was untouched by the turmoil around him, and

who, without even asking, was by some special dispensa-
tion afforded the fierce protection a wild animal will give its
helpless cub, even at the cost of her own life. It wasn't fair,
damn it! Who the hell was this Oostdyk to be so swaddled
in a magic cocoon, taking it for granted, not even aware of
its cozy presence? And not for the first time since the case
had started, he thought that this was no kind of life, when
success became at least as depressing as failure, and a job
well done, a trap so cagily sprung, could bring so little satisfaction to him while others were overwhelmed by misery.
He turned Elfie Von Hesse over to the sergeant on duty
and told him what to do. Then he strode away without
looking at the prisoner again.

He shook his head briskly, as if clearing it of any
doubts or regrets that might inhibit him from going on.
And he *was* going on. Oostdyk was off the hook on this
one, but there was another crime still to be probed, and for
that there was no longer any great-granddaddy's time clock
to provide an airtight alibi. And for that matter, he reminded himself, he'd better look again at Billy Belding and
Carl Van Houten, see if their stories held up for December
fourth the way they did for the fifth; right now he'd prefer
to hang it on Oostdyk, but he knew he was too much of a
cop to let his anger stand in the way of appropriate action.

He went out, slammed the station door behind him,
and got behind the wheel of his car with no notion of where
he was going, except that it would be somewhere away
from here. That was where he was going—away, simply
away.

CHAPTER 32

May 26: White Rose

"**O**H, GOD, COOL it, will you, girl? Just calm down. You said you wanted to help and you did. You helped. You want a murderer should go free because you played bridge with her alternate Saturdays for a couple of hundred years?" Morrison shifted irritably in his seat. "For God's sake," he muttered.

"I know," Harriet said. "But I tricked her. I made her think Henry was going to be arrested. You knew, somehow you knew, she wasn't about to let that happen." She sniffed, and threw yet another sodden tissue into the pail next to the kitchen table, where they were sitting over a pot of tea. She picked up a morsel of coffee cake and looked at it as if it had been guaranteed by the baker to grant unhappiness to the consumer, and bit into it like a child ordered to shut up and eat those brussels sprouts. "How did you know, Hugh?"

"I didn't. I had a hunch. I don't want to talk about it."

"It won't kill you to tell me. You owe me that much."

Morrison frowned. "Okay. I didn't know. Honestly. But I remembered that story you told me about Elfrida

Von Hesse and Henry Oostdyk going around together before he ditched her for the other one. I thought maybe she still had this thing for him, if the story was true. And if it wasn't true, there'd be no harm done. And you told me how she thought the old settler families around here were like only part-time residents, with most of the year spent on Mount Olympus with the rest of the gods. So I thought maybe if I stirred things up . . ."

"You sure did. I did. And I feel sick about it."

"Now you know how it is sometimes being a cop." He took a long, noisy pull on his tea. "Gotta go."

"What's going to happen to her?"

"What do you think's going to happen to her?" he asked harshly. "She'll go to jail, that's what. She killed somebody, no? Ah, what the hell, Harriet, that's the way it has to be. Look, she'll do time, but if she's got a smart lawyer and she behaves herself, she'll be out in three, four years. And they won't stick her in one of the rough places, I promise. My testimony'll make that certain. So she'll run the prison library and make everybody who wants to read a book miserable, and yeah, it's lousy, but yeah, there are worse things on earth. Gotta go."

"All right, Hugh. Give me a call."

Morrison was on his way to Woodstock, where a trendy young painter, one of the darlings of SoHo, had gotten high and piled up his BMW. The major difference between this and any other accident was that an economy-size packet of cocaine was nestling in the wreckage, and the artist was insisting a hitchhiker must have left it on the seat. It was about as likely that Elizabeth Taylor would have misplaced an outsized diamond ring after washing her hands in the lady's loo at the neighborhood Burger King, but the law said something tiresome about presumed innocence, so he was headed up to look into the affair.

At least the drive gave him a chance to think about the Belding case. He had had Pinky get the December 3 passenger manifests for every airline serving San Juan, but

191

Van Houten's name hadn't been there. The man had the most solid alibi of all of them, sitting in the sun and making what Morrison was sure was vast pots of illegal bucks every time he scratched his can. Bill Belding was a pussycat of another color, however. He had indeed been in Boston the nights of the fourth and fifth, leaving on the sixth, but that gave him most of the fourth in New York City, with ample opportunity for driving up to Appleboro, offing dear old dad, and getting back down to La Guardia to board a late-afternoon shuttle. And he couldn't account for his whereabouts on the fourth, though that was in itself evidence of absolutely nothing; there are damn few people, even high-powered top-executive people, whose calendars will show what they were doing all day six months before.

That still left Oostdyk. He had had more opportunity than anyone else to kill Jason Belding, and the possible motives were at least as strong as anyone else's. Maybe even stronger: He needed the money, and the other two only wanted it. It was only his character that was against it. It was more likely he would have threatened Belding and then watched the man die of boredom over a long period of time, years maybe.

And maybe, just maybe, Matilda Jessup. But if it was she, they'd never find out. He sighed. If only a drifter would come forward and say he struck Belding down because his request for eighteen dollars for a cup of coffee had met with a rebuff. Damn it all, anyway.

What Morrison didn't know was that one of his potential killers was about to remove himself from consideration.

"This meatball of a cop has been around again," Billy Belding complained. "He's decided I didn't kill Dad on December fifth, so now he's trying for the fourth! There are only three hundred and goddamn sixty-five days in the year, so this could go on forever. Christ, what an ass!"

"So what'd you tell him?" Georgia asked, patching up a small imperfection in the makeup on her left eyelid. "And what are we seeing tonight?"

"*Don Giovanni*. What could I tell him? I went to Boston that afternoon, and I didn't have any appointments for earlier in the day, so there was nothing on the calendar. I told him I always kept the calendar clear before one of these trips so I can get myself ready, study the papers, crap like that, but what the hell does a stupid cop understand about these things!"

"Oh, I remember. The day you were leaving for Boston. Of course. Why don't you tell him where you were?"

"I told him I was in the office before I left for the plane. But who's going to back me up? Six months ago. Who could remember?"

"No," Georgia said, backing away from the mirror, her left eyelid finally a miracle of loveliness, "I mean tell him where you were besides the office that day. With witnesses and everything. Well," she reconsidered, "one witness anyway. But a good one."

"What are you talking about?"

"I'm talking about I called your office because you forgot to put your shirts in. Left them on top of the dresser when you packed. Your girl told me you had phoned and she said you weren't expected; you were taking a morning flight to Boston, which was about eight hours different from what you told me, sweetyfoot. That's what I'm talking about."

She lifted a comb to touch her hair, which didn't truly need touching. "So I got to thinking. And," she said, turning to look at Billy, "to checking. And I found out. You were at Babydoll's place, weren't you, and after you promised you were finished with that cheap piece of goods."

"Oh."

"You can say that again: Oh. I wasn't going to say anything, but if you need an alibi, and it looks as if you do, there it is. After all, if a husband can't have his wife to lean on when there's trouble, well, what's a marriage all about?

193

Unless, of course, you'd prefer to lean on Miss Babydoll. Well," she wound up, slipping into her coat, "we'd better be off if we don't want to be late. This ought to be useful. Maybe you can pick up a couple of tips from Don Giovanni about doing these things with a little more flair. Less groping about, Billy, you know?"

CHAPTER 33

May 30: Fleabane

"**P**INKY," MORRISON SAID, "next time round I'm going to be a gas-pump jockey. You stick the nozzle in the tank, you turn it on, and the machine figures it out. You get money or you write up a charge, and that's all. No problems. Now I've got some fancy art dealer from New York saying this Woodstock slob is the hope of young America, which it seems proves he couldn't have anything to do with controlled substances, and if he did, which he didn't, it's different for him than for you or me."

"How about spitting on the sidewalk? You allowed to nail him for that? And me, next time around I'm going to be a matinee idol. Money, broads, like that. And lotsa controlled substances that my buddies could say I didn't have anything to do with, leastways till my nose falls off. You think a no-nose matinee idol could make it? It might work: Kinky works these days, hey?"

"Why not? Anyway, Woodstock gets priority. Murder doesn't compute when you put it next to anything that might interfere with the creative output of America's sweetheart, God forbid. The chief says so, the mayor says so, so I guess I say so."

"Me, too. What do you want to do with what I've got on the Belding case?"

"Let me have it. I'll put it with my stuff. It goes into the bottom drawer." He started stacking the papers spread over his desk in preparation for putting them away.

"To from which it'll never emerge."

"Amen. To from which it'll never emerge," Morrison agreed. He held out a hand and Pinky filled it with a smaller sheaf of papers. "Too damn bad," he said and gave them a cursory glance.

At least the glance was cursory until something caught his eye, a name on the United passenger manifest for last December 3, San Juan to New York. Then he turned quickly to the manifest for December 5, New York to San Juan and found another name, a different one, but a name that was equally interesting. He had never met anybody with either name, but it was worth checking up on. One last try.

"Hey, Pinky," he said, "do me a big favor, will you? Call information in Larchmont, see if you can get a number for this guy, will you? And try the phone company in Amityville for this one." He wrote two names on a slip of paper. "That doesn't work, get in touch with the post office both places. This could be nothing, but it could be something hot just as easy."

"My pleasure."

"Thanks, kid. I'd do it myself, but I've got to get up to Woodstock. Everybody who's anybody artwise is waiting for me, and if the chief sees me doing anything else, he'll blow a fuse."

"You want to tell me what it's about?"

"Not yet. This could be stupid. Let's just say that a rose by any other name would smell as bad, if I'm right. Well, I'm off. I may or may not be back with a Ford Foundation grant to erect a minimalist sculpture honoring police brutality at the entrance to a whorehouse, but anyway, I'll be back."

"When?"

"Shit, when I get here, I guess." He shuffled out reluctantly, nearly going backward in his lack of enthusiasm.

And when he did get back, the next morning, Pinky had several items of interest waiting for him: There was no phone for a Carl Leerdam at the listed address in Larchmont or at any other address in Larchmont, and the listed address was a fire station to begin with. As for Amityville, the situation was approximately the same, except that any Mr. Carl Appel, if he had ever lived there, would either be dead or amphibious, since his house number put him a couple of hundred yards out into the Great South Bay or the Atlantic Ocean, depending on how large the intervening lots were.

CHAPTER 34

June 4–5: Sheep Laurel

BY SOME KIND of legalistic magic designed by a Manhattan law firm, orchestrated by well-placed patrons of the arts on the Upper East Side, and crooned like a castrato by an Albany politician eager to live down his often-quoted praise for that great American dramatist Henry Wadsworth Shakespeare, the investigation of the Woodstock case was taken away from the local authorities and given indecently prompt interment in the state capital. The Woodstock community, tired of being identified exclusively with the arts and other forms of sin, was delighted. The state police, with the gloomy foreknowledge that an investigation would leave them stranded with an enhanced reputation for incompetence and art-bashing, were delighted. Senior Investigator Morrison, reluctant at the likelihood he would be required to perform significant modern dances with a spyglass in one hand and a pail of whitewash in the other, was more than delighted. Enraptured would not have been an inappropriate description.

"Poor Hugh," Harriet said, not really understanding the man's pleasure at being removed from a situation almost certain to attract national attention.

"And that's not the worst of it," Morrison said.

"For three days running, I had to eat lunch up there. You know what it's like to eat in an art colony, for God's sake? Don't answer. I'll tell you. Organically grown seeds. Imported Japanese seaweed. Sprouted things like my mother would have thrown out because they had gone bad. Nuts— without salt. Listen, Harriet, next to that garbage, tofu is rare roast beef. I'll never knock tofu again." He paused, contemplating the extent of his sacrifice in the line of duty. "And what have you been doing?"

"The usual. Not much. Does this mean you'll be back on Jason's case?"

"I guess. Along with smashed liquor store windows and drunken driving." He thought about those passenger manifests. "But we're not finished yet, believe me."

"Okay, and remember, anything I can do to help."

"Yeah, sure."

"Meanwhile, I've got some news for you. Henry Oostdyk's been up here to talk about the right-of-way over Jason's land."

Morrison looked surprised. "I thought that was all finished. You said no and you meant no. They ought to get the idea by now, leave you alone."

"It wasn't like that. He wasn't nasty. Henry's really an old sweetie." Her lips tightened. "It's that Judith. She's the one. Henry says he got a developer willing to put up only twenty-five houses, no modulars, all built to individual specs."

"What'd you tell him?"

"I said I'd think about it. What do you think, Hugh? I hate the idea of building anything at all up there. On the other hand, I know Henry needs the money, and God knows the Beldings, the way that Georgia dresses and spends, could use it, too. I don't know what to do."

"You haven't mentioned how Judith Oostdyk feels about it."

"Judith Oostdyk is a stubborn, arrogant bitch and I couldn't care less how she feels about it."

"You sure?"

199

"What's that supposed to mean?"

Morrison sighed. Sometimes cops have to be spiritual advisors and act as if they had an inside line on ethics, morality, and God, sort of a priest without the drag. "Means how much is it that you don't want any construction up the mountain and how much that you enjoy bashing that broad in her well-corseted kazoo. It seems to me I've heard you say you knew people needed housing even if you didn't like to see the town growing so fast. Didn't you say it was only this shoddy suburban tract development you were against? You can't have it both ways. Either you're against bad growth that'll muck up the landscape or you're against growth, period. What do you say?" She said nothing. "And incidentally," Morrison went on, "a little town like this, a body's got to hang on to the friends he's got. You sure you want to cut the Oostdyks out of your life, just for spite? Maybe you could get them to put in a little park, even."

"It's not just for spite." She squirmed uneasily on her seat. "And it'd be another Oostdyk memorial park. Be better if they put in an Oostdyk memorial dump."

"You sure?"

"You sound like a stinking echo, Morrison. Anyway, let's drop it for now. I'll think about it."

"Good. And listen, girl, any way you decide is okay with me. I won't say a damn thing. Okay?"

Harriet smiled. "Yes, Father Morrison."

"That's what I was afraid of. Look, I ought to get home now. I'll be back on the case tomorrow and I want to grab a good night's sleep." He planted a kiss lightly on her forehead and left.

For the first time in a long time, too long a time, Morrison was anxious to get to the station house promptly the next morning. Once at his desk, he whipped out Pinky's notes on the nonexistent Carls, Leerdam and Appel, and dialed a Manhattan number.

"Van Houten Enterprises," a voice sang. "May I help you?"

"Doris?" Morrison asked.

"Miss Sedran isn't with the firm any longer. Can someone else help you?"

"No, this is a personal call. Can you tell me how to get in touch with her?"

There was a moment's hesitation. "I'm sorry, sir, but we're not allowed to give out that kind of information. Can someone else help you?" she repeated.

"I guess not. Thanks a lot."

He considered the options. He could just tell Van Houten he wanted the woman's address, but he'd prefer not to set the hairs on the back of the man's neck twitching. Not yet, anyway. He tried the phone company for all five city boroughs, but with no luck.

Then he had another idea. He turned to Pinky. "Hey, any of the girls on duty this morning?"

"Yeah, I think so. Yeah, Sylvia and Joellen."

Sylvia and Joellen. One too young and pretty for what he wanted, the other looking like an Olympic shot put champion. A nice, elderly, motherly, confidence-inspiring type was what he needed. Harriet? He looked around guiltily as if his thoughts could have been overheard. It wouldn't be strictly by the rules—hell, it wouldn't be even unstrictly by the rules, but if they could twist things around for this painter type in Woodstock, then he could learn from his betters and do the same for Harriet. She wanted to be of help; it was important to her, and he knew how she could do it. There were other ways just as good, but there was nothing wrong with this except for not being regulation.

He dialed. "Harriet, Hugh here. Listen, I've got a job for you if you want it. You can help on the case. Really. Not now; tonight. I can't tell you now, I said. No! Well do you want to help or don't you? Okay, one more crack about leaving notes in the hollow oak next to the cemetery and the whole thing's off, you get me? Okay. Tonight. And we eat at a chophouse. Yes I can, and you can, too. You can order grilled shrimp; chophouses always have grilled shrimp. Stop it. If they can deep-fry shrimp, they can grill them. Okay. I'll pick you up at six. Have a stiff drink for me. Something tells me I'm going to need it. And you want, you can take along a tuna on whole wheat, eat it in the car! Hold the mayo, slap on some yogurt."

Later, after the cannibalized remains of a grilled double pork chop had been removed and they were sitting over the compromise dessert (baked apple, no cream), Morrison finished explaining. "So all you have to do is go to Van Houten's office in Manhattan soon as I'm sure he'll be out of town for a couple of days and ask the secretary. You've got to be ready to take the bus down on short notice, no matter what. There's no need for you to do this at all, Harriet. I can always get someone in the department, but I kind of thought you might like the job yourself."

"Oh, don't you dare get anyone in the department for this. I wouldn't like to do it, I'd love to! This is one I owe to Jason Belding, and if you think Carl Van Houten was involved, I can't think of anything I'd rather do than help you prove it."

"I don't just think it, Harriet. I know it. But I can't prove a damn thing and that's why I need your help. Don't ask me to tell you how I know it, because that's police business. Just trust me."

"That's good enough for me, Hugh."

"And I've got to warn you about one thing. This may all come to nothing. He still could wiggle out, so don't expect miracles."

"Just tell me what to do."

"Nothing but what I've already told you. Yeah, you might see if you have any clothes would make you look like a tourist down in town. I figure a gal like you must have a closetful of print dresses, white shoes, silver-blue hair rinse, colorless nail polish, and all that classy stuff you probably wear to church socials." He grinned.

"Wipe it off, Morrison, before I flatten your face with my matching white plastic pocketbook. Now let's get out of here. I want to practice my act."

C H A P T E R 35

June 8: Purple Vetch

HARRIET DRESSED FRANTICALLY, aiming to catch the ten-thirty bus to town. Hugh had called; Van Houten had left his city office for the opening ceremonies of the new development in North Carolina. Exit the villain; enter Aunt Millie. She looked critically at the blue and white canvas walking shoes excavated from a carton in the attic and tossed them aside. Looking the part was one thing, but overgilding the turkey was quite another. Instead, she slipped into the low-heeled white oxfords she had always hated and studied herself in the full-length mirror on the back of the bathroom door. (It was usually too clouded with steam to see anything in, and these days that was the way she liked it.) The only deviation from Hugh's instructions had been her refusal to use a blue rinse on her hair. She had, after all, a certain amount of pride, and there was no point in encouraging the hens in the supermarket to snigger behind her back over the next Lord knew how many weeks.

Three hours later, she knocked timidly on the door to Van Houten Enterprises. A voice came through the frosted glass instructing her to come in. Clutching her white vinyl bag in both hands, holding it up to her chest, she approached the outer office desk, smiling timidly. "I didn't know whether to knock or just barge in," she said. "Things are so different in New York."

"That's all right, ma'am," the young lady behind the desk said. "What can I do for you?"

"I came in last night from Sedalia and I wanted to surprise my niece. Is she around? Doris, that is. Doris Sedran."

"Oh, I'm sorry, but Doris has left the company. Some weeks back."

"Dear. It was stupid of me not to write, I guess." (She had at first considered saying "I reckon," but decided that Sedalia wasn't really that much of a gallus-snapping backwater.) "I wanted to surprise her. Such a sweet girl, don't you think?"

"I never met her, I'm afraid. I'm sorry. I got here after she was gone."

"Well, it's my own darned fault. I always used to write her here, too, and I haven't the faintest idea where she lives." No assistance being proffered, she tried again. "Could I look at your telephone book, please?" She sat down to study the Manhattan book. "Not here. Maybe I could look at the Brooklyn book? Or have I heard that Brooklyn is all colored people now. Shucks." She looked down at the white gloves clutched in her hand, gloves she had decided on by herself without that bossy Hugh Morrison telling her how these things are done.

There was silence. Harriet sighed wearily. "I should have written," she repeated. "Called even, though I can never get used to using the long-distance phone without feeling guilty. Thank you for your courtesy, Miss. I'll get out of your hair now."

At last. The other woman stirred in her seat, her lips pursed thoughtfully. "Wait a second," she said. "We're not supposed to give out personal information, but heck, I can't see it'll do any harm, a case like this. You just sit yourself right there and I'll check the files for your niece's home address." She sprang up and walked briskly to the row of cabinets against the wall, eschewing, in front of this nice old lady, the rolling lope she favored when Mr. Van Houten was on board.

"Bless you, young lady," Harriet said when she had copied down the information she needed. "I'll be on my way now." And so she was, after a few more appropriate words of thanks and farewell.

To her complete surprise, as she exited the building, she saw Hugh Morrison waiting just beyond the revolving doors. "Land's sake," she cried, "Senior Investigator Morrison. What are you doing here? New York's just a small town after all, isn't it? A body never knows who she's going to run into."

"Let's not get carried away by the performance," Morrison said. "The Act Three curtain's down. Better wait for the reviews."

"Wait, hell. I've got 'em right here." She fished in her bag for Doris Sedran's address. "Take a look at that. Or as we say in Sedalia, feast your glims on this, sonny."

Morrison looked at her in disbelief. "Which Sedalia is that, lady?" He took the slip of paper. "Great work. I'll buy you a drink for this."

"Okay, but with the outfit I'm sporting, it'll have to be a martini in a flowered teacup. Let's go, big boy." They locked arms and sailed down the street triumphantly.

The drink segued into lunch and following that, Morrison said, "Listen, I figure on staying in town and calling the woman after she gets home from work. What say we take in a movie this afternoon and then I'll put you on the bus for home?"

"Fine. Let's make it Radio City Music Hall. We little old ladies from out of town always like the Music Hall. Maybe they've got a Doris Day picture. Such a clean-cut thing, not a bit like most of the kids nowadays!"

"Hey, when are you going to cut this out?"

"I don't know. Maybe never. So far, it's got me a

drink, lunch, and a first-run movie. Let's go, sonny. I'm ten years older than God and I'm set to blast off!"

Morrison's hunch that Doris Sedran was the type to go home after work rather than hit the cocktail circuit was correct. He reached her just before six and explained his need to check a few facts.

"Oh, sure," she said. "I'd ask you up here, but with Manhattan rents what they are, I share the place with a couple of friends. Not much privacy."

"Sure. You pick someplace, a coffee shop, maybe, and I'll meet you there."

Twenty minutes later they were deep in discussion of Van Houten Enterprises. "The pay was good," Doris explained, "but I always felt that Mr. Van Houten figured he was making payments on me personally every time I got my check. I don't mean he tried anything—I wouldn't have interested him that way, anyway—but it was like he had a mortgage on me."

"How do you figure that?"

"It's sort of hard to explain. I'll give you a couple of examples. On my birthday, he'd take me out to a real expensive place. The man's no piker and I've got to hand him that. But he could make a girl feel as if he was doing her a big favor, and he always let me know how much it cost. The two of us would run up, oh, maybe an eighty-dollar tab, and he'd say something like, 'Eighty bucks, Doris. Not bad for a little girl like you, hey?' It was embarrassing. And it made me feel like a pet poodle he brought a big bone home for."

"Sounds rotten."

"It was, believe me." She warmed to the task. "Oh, yeah, and then at Christmas, he'd give me too much, like an expensive pin, and wait for me to show gratitude, and even worse, he'd let me know what he'd like. Of course, it didn't cost as much as what he gave me, but it would be something more than I could afford anyway, like a fancy pen and pencil set, and he knew it. You know, I never thought of it this way before, but it was like tribute to the lord of the manor."

"That fellow in your office, Chris Morton, he get the same treatment?"

"He sure did. He was smarter than me, though. He didn't wait for the boss to get tired of kicking him around, the way I did. Chris got himself a better job down in Lauderdale."

"There's something else more important I want to ask you about, Miss Sedran." She nodded. "Would there be any reason for the boss to sneak back from an out-of-town trip sometimes, I mean without putting it on the books, maybe using a fake name for the airline ticket, then go off again?"

"Oh, sure. All the time."

"What's the point?"

"Well, you know officially his home's in Connecti-cut. That means that he doesn't have to pay New York resi-dent income taxes any days he doesn't work in the New York office. The headquarters is here in Manhattan, but he travels a lot, and when he's on the road, the New York taxes on him get cut way down. So if he's on a trip and wants to come back for a couple of days, he sneaks in with-out putting it on the books." She looked up hopefully. "You think the tax boys will get him? Gee, I wouldn't mind that a bit."

"I wish I could say so, but right now there's some-thing else I'm working on. Were there any particular names he'd use on the airline tickets when he pulled this kind of thing?"

"Gee, I couldn't tell you. He played it very close to the chest. Chris Morton would probably know because he handled the books more than I did, but I can't help with that. I'm sorry."

"Don't be sorry. You've been a great help and I thank you."

207

"Believe me, the pleasure is all mine. It's my own fault I stayed with him so long. I didn't have to be that miserable for over three years, but I was, and maybe it's mean of me, but I just hope the SOB gets whatever's coming to him."

"He will, Miss Sedran, he will. I think I can promise you that." He thanked her and left, first getting the name of Chris Morton's firm in Florida so he could call him in the morning. I can hardly wait, he told himself happily.

CHAPTER 36

June 9: Spurge

"**L**ISTEN, MR. MORTON," Morrison said into the phone, "there's nothing for you to worry about. I'm not interested in what you yourself did or didn't do, and I don't work for the state tax people. Look. The man who was blocking your boss's project in Appleboro was murdered. That's what I'm working on. Period. That's all I care about. Okay? I don't give a damn how Van Houten or you or anybody else cooked the books, you understand?"

"Yeah, that's what you say, but how do I know what you mean? What am I, dumb? I'm not playing fall guy for Carl Van Houten, I promise you."

"Let's put it this way. Either you take my word for it, I'm only concerned with Van Houten, or else I hop on my tricycle up to the tax boys in Albany and give them a couple of hot tips. You read me? Wouldn't do much for you with your present employer, either."

"Okay, so I've got no choice. I've got your word for it, huh? Yeah, you're right. He was in and out of town like a yoyo sometimes. One trip he'd be Carl Appel for the airlines, others he'd be Carl Leerdam, like that vase in the reception room."

"Why not something simple, like Smith?"

"You tell me. The way I see it, it made him think he was thumbing his nose at the government, sort of giving them hints they'd be too dumb to catch on to. Big shotitis, and he had a real case, believe me."

"So I've heard. Did he assign you presents to buy him, too, like Doris? Tokens of your respect and admiration?"

"Did he ever! Last Christmas, silver nail file and clippers, and it had to be monogrammed. Three initials cost extra, as he damn well knew. The one he lost wasn't even monogrammed at all except on the case, which is a hell of a lot cheaper. Year before that, monogrammed military brushes. He was big on monograms. Like to put his mark on everything, I guess, starting with Doris and me. Listen, you sure I'm going to be all right? You taping this or something?"

Morrison laughed. "Relax. You've been watching too much television. One day I may need a sworn statement from you that he traveled in and out of town under an alias, but that's where it stops. I told you, you play ball with me, I play ball with you. Now you go out to lunch down there and have yourself a stiff drink. That's what I'm going to do up here. You ought to feel pretty good, man; you got something off your chest, and maybe you helped the law pin a no-good to the wall. Good citizen stuff."

"Yeah, I guess. I'm going to have a frozen daiquiri; it's hot in Lauderdale. How about you?"

"You just blew it, pal. I've got a lot to get through today, so just a beer, a small one. So long now." He laughed. "See you in court."

Later, Morrison went out with Pinky to the Route 44 deli. He carried his corned beef on rye, lots of mustard, a side of fries, and a can of Bud out to one of the tables set up on the deck for the warm weather. Pinky followed suit, though with breast of turkey; the man was nursing an ulcer. "So how's it going?" Pinky asked. "You got a shit-eating grin on your face, man. What's up?"

"Plenty. But not enough. I've got Van Houten back in New York when Belding was killed. Not in San Juan, buddy. In New York."

"Nice. But that's still no smoking gun in his hand."

"Don't tell me. I know." He lifted the can of beer to his lips and let the cool liquid flow down his throat. "But if I got him all the way back from San Juan, damn it, a couple thousand miles almost, I can get him seventy-five more to Appleboro. Somehow he's left a trail. He's too happy with how smart he is, how stupid everybody else is. There's something there to find, and," he finished, thinking of Harriet, "I'm going to find it."

"Gasoline credit charges? Entries in a bankbook? Maybe somebody in his office could know?"

"We'll check it all, but the guy's no dummy. It's not going to be a walkover."

"Somewhere along the line, he's dropped a couple of stitches, let his guard down. It's gotta be that way." Pinky, looking glumly at Morrison's beer, sipped his ulcer delight, a container of milk.

"Easy to say." They sat quietly. Then Morrison said, very softly, "Man, you just did it. That's it. He dropped a couple of stitches. And that's not all. We've got him, boy! You did it!"

Pinky blinked. "I did? If you say so. So tell me more."

"Wait a second. This calls for a celebration." He went inside and extracted a can of beer and a carton of milk from the refrigerator case. "Have another champagne, son. This one's on me."

"Too much," the other man murmured.

"S'nothing. Look. What'd Morton say about the Christmas present he had to give Van Houten last year? I'll tell you. He said he had to give the boss monogrammed nail file and clippers, the initials on the silver, and that it was a replacement for the clippers the man lost. Right?"

"Right. So?"

"So first thing, the lost clippers had a monogram on the leather case, not directly on the silver. And they were lost *before* Christmas last year. Which means that when Belding's son conned him into moving the body this spring, he couldn't have lost them then. He dropped them long before, like on December fourth, when he snuck up from Puerto Rico to New York and snuck up from New York to Appleboro.

"Maybe they took a walk, looked at the property together. Hell, I don't know. Maybe Van Houten tried to talk the guy into seeing things his way. Maybe they had a fight and he didn't mean to kill the man. I don't know. Probably we'll never know. But accident or on purpose, he did it. Carl Van Houten killed Jason Belding and left him out there on that field. And, by God, we've got that silver gizmo out there long before Christmas to prove it. So when this guy in Van Houten's office gave him a new one, he didn't just give a present to Van Houten—"

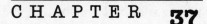

CHAPTER 37

October 12: Frost, and the Leaves Have Turned

"—bUT HE GAVE a present to us, too. Case of a guy so pleased with how smart he is that he trips himself up." He poured two more martinis from the pitcher Harriet had taken out to the terrace, and looked down the hill from his chair. The maples were scarlet and orange and gold; the dogwood was deep wine; the birches and aspen and hickory a bright yellow. Only the stubborn oaks were nasty brown holdouts. "This weekend's going to be peak color."

"Mm. Let's drive up the mountain Sunday."

"Too many tourists. How about Monday?"

"Don't you have to be in the office?"

Morrison shrugged. "Screw the office. I've done enough for them lately. Monday?"

"Sure. Monday, then. You sound pretty pleased with yourself, Hugh."

"I suppose I am. We couldn't prove it wasn't an accident, the way Van Houten claims, and frankly, I kind of think maybe it *was* an accident. Guy like Van Houten doesn't set out to kill, but he gets damned mad when he can't get his way. He probably hit Jason Belding too hard, then got scared and beat it the hell back to Puerto Rico, but fast."

Harriet's voice was faint. "He says Jason tripped, that he didn't lay a finger on him."

"What did you expect him to say? But the jury believed otherwise. Anyway, manslaughter will keep him inside a couple of years. It's over, Harriet."

They sat quietly. The breeze rustled through the trees and the first dead leaves of autumn tumbled through the air like flocks of drunken blue jays. The sun, no longer the burning yellow of summer, blanketed the hillside with an icy white gold.

Morrison cleared his throat. "Uh, look, Harriet. I suppose now that the case is closed, there's no need for me to be up here as much as before, huh?"

"Are you out of your mind, Morrison? What are you, a shy adolescent, worried about pimples?" Then she added, almost inaudibly, "More need than ever, Hugh, believe me. Besides," she finished, sitting straight up, "now that I've finally weaned you from beer and got you on to civilized drinking, don't you dare walk out on me."

They turned toward each other and grinned, two conspirators plotting friendship.

Morrison lifted his glass. "A loaf of bread, a jug of low-fat milk, and thou beside me," he said.

Harriet returned the salute. "Absolutely stinking in the wilderness," she said.

Postscript

HUGH MORRISON WAS wrong about one thing: It wasn't over. Not quite. There was further retribution awaiting Carl Van Houten, though it was dispensed by a Higher Authority than the criminal-justice system. He served out three years of his sentence, but in addition, he contracted hepatitis, which, as best as anybody could figure, came from drinking contaminated water at one of his housing developments shortly before he went to prison. That it was a development to which an ecologically minded band of troublemakers had objected, claiming the wells and septic tanks were too close together for safety, may or may not have been a coincidence.

The illness left him permanently enervated, and after release, he found he lacked the drive to reestablish himself as a legal crook. Ultimately, he opened a small real estate office a little north of Appleboro and sold weekend cabins to city people laboring under the delusion that they could reclaim a lost innocence (which, to begin with, many of them had never possessed) through owning a dollop of God's sacred soil.

The Oostdyks, with Harriet's acquiescence, sold their land to a developer more temperate in his greed than

215

Carl Van Houten, which got them on their financial feet once more and enabled Judith in particular to pursue her destiny as the chief source of grace and favor in Appleboro. (Her bridge games, however, lacking Elfie, Jason, Ben, and now Harriet were never re-established as a major social phenomenon of the Appleboro season.)

Billy and Georgia Belding were equally pleased. The infusion of funds into their joint bank account made possible by the sale of a right-of-way to the new development provided a respite of several years from having to consider the extent to which outlay was exceeding income. They soared to an emotional plateau that they both looked on as relative marital content, never once becoming aware that true content is qualitatively different from the calm produced by a balance of terror.

Matilda Jessup passed the rest of her days in a mental hospital, waiting for her husband, waiting for her son, neither happy nor unhappy. Only waiting.

Elfie Von Hesse was found not guilty by reason of temporary insanity. She was, however, incarcerated until such time as the state psychiatrists declared that they had restored her to mental health, which was a lie, though an unwitting one. (Of course what they meant was that they considered her at last to be a dull normal, precisely the way the psychiatrists were themselves.) She moved to Minneapolis, where she opened, and ran with an iron hand, an employment service dedicated to finding jobs for women who had served time in prison before being thrown back into society.

Elsa Neiswender's mother spent her last years largely in attending the funerals of her contemporaries, the ride to the cemetery being one of her few sources of genuine pleasure. One particular outing afforded her more pleasure than her brittle frame could accommodate, and she expired, exhausted but happy. Miss Neiswender thereupon married her gentleman friend of many years, abandoning her position as secretary to Mr. McCollum, principal of the middle school, to a younger single woman. Mr. McCollum had, however, overlooked the fact that single women often have brothers, and the second time that he leaned over the woman's shoulder to help her with her artwork, the brother went into the school and thrashed the hapless man soundly, to the delight of the student body, an assortment of visitors, and the former Miss Neiswender.

Melvin Spingle grew up, despite the lack of approbation from his father, his teachers, or the local police, and at the age of nineteen published his first book of imaginary happenings, *Spooks by Spingle.* This was followed by *More Spooks by Spingle,* an even greater success. His father, though without conscious realization, was terribly annoyed by Melvin's triumphs but was able to assuage his upset by switching from beer to bourbon, thanks to his son's generosity.

Merwin Brotz, D.D.S., never was able to afford a nurse to serve as a buffer between his work and the demands of the telephone; since Appleboro wasn't doing much growing, neither was his practice. He moved to suburban Philadelphia, and within a few years had a practice staffed with personable young ladies in white smocks, a veritable stable of good cheer and efficiency, looking like an army of supermarket clerks and indeed possessing the same degree of knowledge of the wonderful world of dentistry as supermarket clerks. Their salaries were built into his charges.

Bob Pettit grew into his role as Appleboro's pet police officer, and with time became more avuncular, entertaining the children of the town, as long as he could make them sit still for it, with tales of derring-do pertaining to his triumphant solution of Appleboro's two most famous, and only, murders.

Smitty the postmaster went on through the years with little change, ever apprehensive about the consequences of upsetting Dolly's nervous stomach, and just a shade jealous of the expanding empires of his fellow

217

postmasters in the burgeoning principalities surrounding Appleboro.

Harriet Lorimer and Hugh Morrison remained friendly and came to depend on each other's company. Hugh, under Harriet's unblinking eye, lost ten pounds on a more or less permanent basis, though with serious remissions during holiday seasons. Harriet, herself, took off five pounds, not because she needed to but because she thought she looked better that way. And she did. Sometimes Hugh stayed overnight, but no one was entirely sure, despite the talk, of what that signified. And nobody dared ask.

And then there was the town of Appleboro, Appleboro itself. It remained steadfastly unAmerican. It failed to grow. The big city to the south spread furiously up and around it like a raging torrent, bringing with it not the usual detritus that accompanies a flood but shopping malls, discount centers, four-lane highways, E-Z payment auto marts, fast-food outlets, garbage, polluted air, ten-story buildings, toxic waste, overloaded landfills, traffic lights, noise, bad tempers, and a generation of inhabitants unaware of their neighbors' names.

In the midst of this, Appleboro remained as an island, untouched by the furious activities that swept by it. There was a story by a latter-day Melvin Spingle about a benevolent witch who once lived on East Mountainside Road and who chased away the bad boys and cast a spell so that all bad-boy buildings that went up during the day were consumed at night by the genie who dwelled in the magic septic tank below. And while nobody could be said to have lived happily ever after, at least their opportunities for so doing were considerably enhanced.